7-4-08

Best Wishes

James Campbell

Luther's Mule

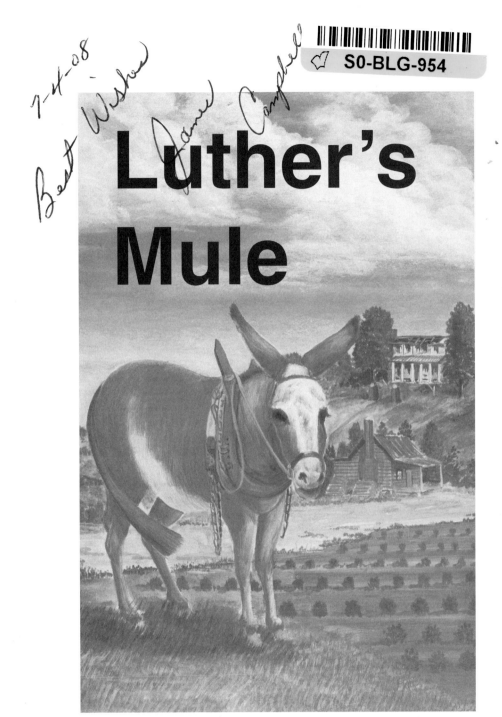

JAMES CAMPBELL

ISBN: 978-1-891029-14-1

Second Printing 2004
Third Printing 2005
Fourth Printing 2007

For other books by James Campbell,

visit:

www.jamescampbellbooks.com

or works by many other

Appalachian Authors,

visit:

www.appalachianauthorsguild.com

HENDERSON PUBLISHING

811 Eva's Walk, Pounding Mill, VA 24637

James T. Campbell

About the Author

James Campbell was born in 1944, during World War II and grew up near the foothills of Big A Mountain in Russell County, Virginia. His life was not easy during that period and he was continually driven to overcome the hardships that his family faced. He was the eldest son of five children, so most of the work, required on the eighty-acre farm, became his responsibility. During his four high school years, he did most of the farm chores in the evenings after school and at night, if there was a full moon.

Many times, while working on the rocky hillside farm where he was raised, he likened it to how the black people must have lived during slavery times. Often times, as he worked, he prayed that God would give him the knowledge to do something other than farm. He will always be thankful to Him that his prayers have, at last, been answered.

He lives with his wife, Margaret, in Tazewell County, Virginia, where they raised their two children, who have both married and moved away from home.

James now spends most of his time writing, the thing he enjoys most, outside of spending time with his family.

Dedication

This book is dedicated to the memory of my brother-in-law, Sherman D. Lowe, who, for many years encouraged me to have my writings published. I regret that he was called from this life without ever knowing that I, at last, found the courage to follow his advise and have my first novel printed.

....And to my daughter, Pamela and son, Jim, Jr., whom I consider to be my greatest contribution to this life.

Appreciation

I will always be grateful to Ken Henderson, of Henderson Publishing, who so patiently worked with me in getting this book published. Without his help, this novel could never have become a reality.

Thank you, Ken.

Table of Contents

Chapter One
The War Takes A Toll

The warm Georgia sun had fallen far down into the western sky as if to be getting ready to settle in for the night. Its last rays lengthened the shadows of the tall sycamore trees upon the gentle flowing waters of the Oconee River. The huge bullfrogs that lived along her banks were beginning to exercise their deep voices.

Far in the distance could be heard the roar of the Macon-to-Atlanta freight train. It would take at least half an hour for it to pass the river bend, and again, be far enough away until it could no longer be heard.

Joe Ray and Luther knew this very well, because they spent many days fishing at the bend of the river during their childhood.

Joe Ray Franklin was the son of a once-wealthy plantation owner. Now, at the age of eighteen, he could hardly

1

remember the glorious days his father often spoke of before the Civil War, which ended ten years ago.

The only thing Joe Ray could remember about this tragic period was that the strain of being reduced to poverty, had caused the death of his mother. He could not even remember her very well, because she was always busying herself with the preparation of some ball or other festive event, leaving him to be cared for by Mattie, his "nanny", who was also Luther's mother.

Luther was the only son born to "Ole Ben" and Mattie Johnson, who were a Negro couple who stayed on the Franklin plantation after the end of the war, even though the end of the war brought an end to their slavery. Luther, like Joe Ray, had been born to his parents after they passed middle age, and also, like his white childhood friend, could remember very little of the happenings before or during the great dispute between the North and South.

Since the end of the war and the death of his mother, Joe Ray's father became less and less interested in any of the goings on around him. He sold off section after section of what was once a large plantation, until it was reduced to a small farm of a mere three hundred acres.

The remains of what had once been their large plantation home still stood, half burned, among a grove of gigantic oak trees on a rise about a hundred yards from the slave-quarter shack Joe Ray and his father called home.

Many times after supper, Joe Ray would wander up to the old mansion and sit until dark, trying to visualize what life would be like if there had not been a war. He often dreamed of earning enough money to buy back the land and return the plantation mansion to its original state. To someday restore the home, he knew was a possibility, but to rebuy the land was unlikely. Each time his father sectioned off another portion to be sold, it was always purchased by John McClanahan, the southern gentleman who owned the adjacent plantation.

Although many of the plantations were destroyed during General Sherman's march to the sea, a handful of them had been spared by him and his Union soldiers. The McClanahan place was one of those left almost untouched.

This was what tortured William Franklin most; probably even more than his own devastation. The grief caused by the loss of his wife passed with time, but when John McClanahan began buying up the land he was forced to sell, William Franklin's resentment for his neighbor grew worse.

Every year since the war, William vowed to rebuild his own vast empire, but each year, the task became more difficult. Most of his hardships began immediately after the fighting stopped. When the Confederacy surrendered, William lost all but a handful of the slaves he so badly needed to carry on the efficient operation of his cotton plantation. Of course, not all the slaves left, but so few remained, the only recourse was to hire the work that needed to be done.

By the end of the first crop year, virtually all the Franklin savings were depleted. This was due to the poor production of the newly freed slaves he was able to hire and the extremely low prices he received from his half-tended crop of cotton.

By the end of the second year, William had to borrow money to even get his seed into the ground. When picking time came, he hoped to be fully recovered financially, but when harvest was over, he was to learn that his situation had only worsened. His only recourse was to sell off a portion of the plantation and start over.

The next half-dozen years brought little change and thus, the once large plantation grew smaller and smaller, as if it were a huge mound of sand, being washed away by a down-pouring rain. As the size of the plantation became smaller, so did William's dreams of rebuilding. Finally, he gave up and became content to spend most of his time just sitting in front of their old slave shack, talking of things that might have been.

Joe Ray had long since grown tired of hearing about their hard times and so, spent much of his time finding other things to occupy his time, like fishing with Luther on the banks of the Oconee River.

Unlike Franklin's place, the McClanahan plantation had flourished, even during the years immediately following the war. Too, William Franklin had only one son, whereas McClanahan had fathered four male offspring that helped him manage his estate.

John McClanahan was somewhat older than Franklin with acquired riches second to few other plantation owners in the whole state of Georgia. Thus, he was more able to withstand the pitfalls of the war and still maintain more than just a comfortable standard of living.

The war had been no picnic for the McClanahans,

but the two sons that were in battle returned home without loss of limb and almost all of the plantation was untouched. And too, when the war ended, many more of his slaves remained on the plantation for fear they could not make it on their own. So, when the Franklin land was sold, he was able to purchase it, thereby adding to the size of his already enormous holdings.

The only daughter born to John and Charlotte McClanahan was Charlene, a beautiful, golden-haired, true southern miss, about the same age as Joe Ray.

Many were the times Joe Ray let himself ponder Charlene's beauty when he was alone in his daydreaming fantasy world.

Thus was the case on this warm September evening as he lounged on the banks of the Oconee River only a few feet away from his Negro friend, Luther.

"You gonna let de biggest ole catfish in these waters pull yo' pole plum down to de 'Lantic Ocean fo' you jerk," Luther yelled.

Luther's statement brought Joe Ray out of his daydreaming and started him scampering down the river bank to grab his fishing pole. No sooner had he picked up his pole than he realized that for once, Luther might be telling the truth. He surely believed he had hooked the largest catfish in the Oconee River. He managed to pull the huge catfish within three feet of the bank before he heard the loud crack of his reed. Within the time it takes to blink your eye, the large fish was gone and most of Joe Ray's fishing pole with it, leaving Joe Ray with only the butt end of his reed still in his hand.

For the next several minutes, Joe Ray just stared in disbelief, letting his anger build, while Luther rolled and hollered and laughed and cut a shine like he had never seen man, or animal either for that matter, do in his life.

Finally, Luther regained enough composure to begin needling Joe Ray.

"What yo' doin' wif dat club in yo' hand, Joe Ray? he asked. "Yo' plannin' on wadin' out in de river an' knockin' one of dem fish in de head?"

"No," yelled Joe Ray. "I'm planning on knocking me a black boy in the head if he don't stop that infernal laughing."

"Shucks, iffen I'd had dat big ol' monster on my fancy new pole, I'd of drug him plum up yonder to de railroad tracks," Luther continued.

"Yeah, and the reason you ain't catching no fish is because you stole that fancy fishing pole the last time you were in Dublin," Joe Ray reminded him.

"I never stole no fishin' pole in my whole life," explained Luther. "I jus" stole myself a new fishin" line an' de pole jus' happen to be on one end of it."

With that, they both started laughing and began walking up toward the railroad tracks to where they left Sadie Mae, Luther's ole mule. The last glow of daylight was giving way to darkness. They had just about reached home, when Joe Ray broke the silence with a question.

"Is it true you stole this old mule?" he asked Luther.

"No," came Luther's quick answer. "I jus' meant to

steal the bridle. It waren't my fault iffen de mule wuz still wearin' it."

"You got to be the laziest, lyingest, stealingest black feller in the whole state of Georgia, Luther," Joe Ray exclaimed as he slid down off the mule.

"Don' yo' tell nobody, Joe Ray, but I shore am workin' at hit," Luther grinned. "Say, when we goin' back down on de river fishin', agin?"

"Day after tomorrow, 'bout noon, I suppose.. Good night, Luther." He added, "And remember, the next time you do some stealing, I'm the one that needs a new pole."

Joe Ray stood in front of his place until he saw Luther disappear into the fallen-down old barn at the far end of the row of shacks.

As Joe Ray approached their quarters, he could see his father sitting on one end of the run-down porch. He was in his regular resting place. Each day, about dusk, William would seat himself in an old hickory bark, straight-backed chair at the south end of their shack. He always tilted the chair back against the wall, lit up his pipe and waited for some of the Negro men to come by.

Most evenings, Ole Ben or some of the other half-dozen men who stayed on after the war would congregate at the Franklin shack. This was one of those evenings.

Their conversations would usually begin with their accomplishments of the day, which were usually very little. But, they always ended on the topic of how things were before the war. Oh, there were a few bales of cotton grown each year, which was enough to pay the taxes on the few

7

acres that were left and to buy food for their tables, but very little more.

The Negroes still called William "Boss Bill" as they had done when they were slaves. But now, they did so out of respect, not because they felt he was their superior.

Boss Bill no longer supervised the Negroes as he did when whey were slaves, but out of sheer need for survival, had become their equal. The crop of cotton, as it was, was grown collectively, and the monitary yield was shared equally.

There was space used each year to grow vegetables, but the men had little to do with this. This task was done by Mattie and the other Negro women.

Mattie was the self-appointed overseer of the growing, canning, preserving, and storing of the garden produce for as long as anyone could remember. And well she should be, for her skills in these matters were second to none. It was truly the garden that sustained life on the plantation, not the income from the cotton. Survival was a joint effort. It could be said that each did his fair share. That is, everyone except Joe Ray and Luther.

Joy Ray, being the only child born to the Franklins, and having lost his mother at such an early age, had been mothered by the Negro women, and excused from manual labor. Mattie took him under her wing when his mother passed away and saw to it that he was treated as one of the South's favorite sons.

Luther, on the other hand, was just plain lazy. Being three years older than Joe Ray, he was appointed guardian,

8

allowing Mattie and the other women to have time for gardening and work in the fields. This arrangement suited Luther just fine. While the others were busy with the chores, Luther and Joe Ray spent their time fishing on the Oconee River, or just plain goofing off. Even as the years passed and Joe Ray became old enough to take care of himself, Luther never let go, for he knew very well that hanging around with Joe Ray was his ticket to the easier life.

The two young men needed little more than what the small plantation provided, but whenever they did, Luther could always find a way to obtain it without working; like the time he decided they needed a canoe. Luther would get out of bed after everyone had gone to sleep and steal vegetables from the garden and hide them until the next day. Then, while the others were at work, he'd take them into Dublin and sell them to anyone who could pay. Before long, he had the money to purchase the canoe.

Joe Ray never participated in any of Luther's dishonest endeavors, but he was forced to cover for him on numerous occasions. He also knew that someday, this stealing would get Luther into big trouble. But, he did not want to think of Luther's problems right now, for he had one of his own.

Tomorrow was Friday, and that was the only day he could visit Charlene.

Joe Ray crossed the porch where his father and the other men were gathered, without even acknowledging their presence. He headed straight to the back room used for their kitchen. He knew that in the warming closet of their wood-burning stove, his supper would be waiting. Suppertime seldom found him home, so when he was not there to eat with the others, Mattie made sure he would not have to go to bed hungry.

When he finished his meal, he joined the men on the porch, not at all interested in what was being said, for he had heard this conversation many times. But, he did want to sit in the moonlight and enjoy the coolness of the evening before going to bed. He seated hmself a few feet away from the others and became lost in his own thoughts about his upcoming day with Charlene.

The next morning, like every other Friday morning, Joe Ray was out of bed bright and early. He collected his best clothes from the dresser on the far side of the room where he knew Mattie would have them washed, folded and ready for him. With his garments in hand, he stepped out onto the porch with only a towel around his midsection. He hesitated for a moment when the morning air hit him. The sun was not yet up to burn away the dampness of the fog which chilled his body. After taking a moment to adjust, he moved from the porch and headed for the back of their shack, where a large porcelean tub was waiting for him.

Joe Ray laid his clothes on a shelf attached to the dwelling. He secured two bricks under one corner of the tub, where a leg was missing, and began moving the handle on the pump to catch his bath water. When there was enough water in the tub, Joe Ray hung burlap sacks around three sides that were not hidden by the shack.

As he placed one foot into the cold water, he thought to himself, "If there is any part of seeing Charlene I don't like, this has to be it." When he finished his bath, in as hurried a manner as possible, he dressed and went back inside where he knew breakfast would be waiting.

Breakfast was the only meal Joe Ray and Boss Bill shared. His father took his noonday meals with Ole Ben and Mattie, or some of the other Negro families. At that time of day, Joe Ray was usually off somewhere with Luther, fishing, or into some other worthless endeavor.

He usually got home in the evenings, long after the others had eaten, but his father always prepared their breakfast. Their meal this morning was not unlike most others they shared, consisting of ham, grits, fried eggs and homemade biscuits from Mattie's kitchen.

Joe Ray wondered how he and Boss Bill could survive if it were not for Mattie. Since President Lincoln had freed the slaves, the Negroes could have gone anywhere they chose. And most of them did, but not Ole Ben and Mattie. Like the others who remained on the plantation, they were in their sunset years.

So, out of respect for the kind treatment Boss Bill had always shown them, and their love for Joe Ray, they chose to stay. Or, maybe it was because they were afraid of what life would offer somewhere else. Whatever the reason, Joe Ray was truly thankful.

After he consumed a manly portion of the food his father set before him, Joe Ray went outside to make plans for the day.

It was still early. Too early to go to the McClanahan plantation. So, he ambled along in front of the row of shacks to where Mattie, Ole Ben and Luther lived. He found Luther sitting on the edge of their front porch with what looked like a worn-out map in his hand.

"What you got there, Luther?' Joe Ray asked as he approached the shack.

"Mornin' Joe Ray. Dis heah's a picture of de whole state of Georgia," Luther answered.

"What are you doing with that, Luther? You planning on stealing the lower half of the state and sellin' it to Florida?"

"Hell no!," cried Luther. "I'm plannin' on us takin' a trip. Talkin' 'bout stealin', I can tell de way yo' all spruced up, dis mus' be Friday. Dat means yo' goin' over to de 'Clanahan's place to steal a little o' Miss Charlene's sugar. Yo' shore can't go this early. De freight train ain't run yet."

Joe Ray knew this was a true fact.

Charlene's father did not approve of Joe Ray seeing his daughter. In fact, the one time he caught Charlene talking to him, he became outraged. He and Charlene were standing outside the church building one evening after Sunday night services and upon seeing them, Mr. McClanahan issued a public reprimand.

"No son of a broke, washed-up, has-been plantation owner is good enough for my daughter," he declared.

Thus, began the weekly secret visits. On Friday of every week, John McClanahan and his missus would ride their carriage down to Dublin, one of the watering

12

stations,where they would catch the train to Macon. They were gone the entire day, which left Joe Ray free to visit Charlene without fear of being caught. He knew they were safe until her folks returned on the train late in the afternoon.

Joe Ray always walked the mile and a half to the McClanahan's place. There were three or four pretty good saddle horses still on their farm, and one run-down carriage. But, he never used them for fear that he could not leave them where they would not be seen by some of the work hands on John's plantation.

At last, it was time to go.

"See you later," he said to Luther.

"Sho' 'nuff, Joe Ray," Luther answered. "An' don't yo' get so lovesick yo' can't go fishin' t'morrow."

Chapter Two
A Day With Charlene

Joe Ray arrived at his and Charlene's regular meeting place just moments before she arrived. They met at this same grove of oak trees, near the southern-most end of the McClanahan plantation for the past year. There were two old storage buildings hidden among the trees that had not been used for years. So, the young couple felt safe here.

Joe Ray would probably have never known about this hideaway were it not for Mattie. She knew how fond the two were of each other and how much the incident at the church had destroyed Joe Ray. Since she and Ole Ben attended the same church meeting, as did the Negro people from the McClanahan plantation, she decided this could not be. Mattie arranged for Sara, one of the McClanahan Negro servants, whom she had known for years, to bring Charlene to this place on a Friday, when her folks were in Macon. From then on, they met each week.

Sara would bring Charlene to the grove as soon as the McClanahans were gone and return for her before time for them to be back home.

Today, Charlene arrived with her usual picnic basket, but they hardly said hello before Joe Ray realized something wasn't just right.

She could not hide her radiant beauty. Even at her worst, she was the most gorgeous lady Joe Ray had ever seen. Charlene, almost eighteen, had fully blossomed into a young lady. She possessed character and features that made her the envy of many of the other Southern belles. Her long blonde hair that she always allowed to flow free, enhanced every other motion of her body. And those blue eyes could ignite the fires of excitement in anyone of the opposite sex, married or single. But, today she lacked the glow of excitement that was so much a part of her.

"Want to tell me what's bothering you?" Joe Ray inquired, as they seated themselves against the trunk of one of the huge oak trees.

"Oh, its just awful," Charlene began to sob. "Father has made arrangements for me to go up to Atlanta to a finishing school. He insists I should learn to become the refined lady some wealthy southern gentlemen would want to wed. I will be gone for a whole year, Joe Ray, and its so far away. But, there is no way I can tell him it is you that I want to marry."

Her statement fell upon Joe Ray's ears with such force, he was in a state of shock and disbelief. Anger began to build inside him and this foreign object in the pit of his

16

stomach strained at every fiber of his being.

Year after year, Charlene's father bought the land that meant so much to him, and now, without knowing it, he was driving a wedge between him and the one person that meant more to him than life itself.

At every meeting for the past year, the two talked of nothing except the time when they would be married. They dreamed of the life they would have together and the plantation they would own; just like the one the war so unmercifully stole from Joe Ray's family. And, even though they made no plans of how all this was to come, they knew that someday it would be.

They knew also that their marriage would have to wait until Charlene became of age because her father would go to his grave before he would ever consent. And even then, Charlene knew she would lose her share of the great wealth her father possessed.

The thought of beginning their lives together penniless, never bothered Joe Ray, but the thought of not being able to see her for a whole year was almost more than he could bear.

"When are you supposed to leave?" he asked, as he blinked back his own tears, trying not to let Charlene detect any sign of weakness.

"In two weeks," was her reply. "Father insists that I can learn no more from the private tutor he hired, and I must leave at once."

The remainder of the day was spent in near silence. Neither could find the words to erase the sadness in their hearts.   17

When Sara returned for Charlene later in the afternoon, she found them holding hands and not saying a word.
The food she had prepared for their picnic was still untouched.

Joe Ray helped Charlene into the buggy beside Sara
and they rode off without either of them uttering a word.

Joe Ray watched as the buggy disappeared from view
and then seated himself back against the same tree where he
and Charlene spent the afternoon. The moon was high before he lifted himself up and began the walk back to his
home.

Chapter Three
Does Joe Ray Measure Up?

That night, sleep for Joe Ray did not come. He could not comprehend how life would be like for a whole year without Charlene. For the first time, he began to compare himself to her and in every category, he believed he fell short.

She was taught to read and write by her mother early in life and the tutor instilled in her many more educational needs. She wore the finest clothes, and she and her family were invited to every social gathering for miles around. She had beauty and all the material things money could buy.

Joe Ray, on the other hand, barely had enough to hold body and soul together. This had never bothered him before, but now, it seemed to be of utmost importance. He decided if he and Charlene were to have a life together, he must make some changes.

Would she meet someone in Atlanta who would steal her away? He had never thought of Charlene and anyone else before, but now the very idea of this happening filled him with fear.

What did she see in him, anyway, he questioned. Sure, he was a handsome young man, he thought. At least, that was what Mattie and the other Negro women were always telling him. He was large for his age with wavy jet-black hair, which was usually too long and fell down on his broad shoulders.

His clothes were always clean. Mattie saw to that, but they never seemed to fit. No sooner would Mattie make the necessary alterations, than he outgrew everything again. The negative thoughts Joe Ray never knew before, kept him awake until dawn. He welcomed the sunrise with enthusiasm. Funny, he thought, how bad things seem even worse when surrounded by darkness.

He was out of bed at first light and could hardly wait for Boss Bill to put breakfast on the table. He hadn't even remembered to eat his supper the night before.

As he ate his breakfast, he began to question Boss Bill. "How much money you got, Daddy?" he asked. Joe Ray had never asked anything like this of his father before, but he knew that in order for him and Charlene to be together, he would need to have cash.

"Not very much," was Boss Bill's answer. "There's enough to put out the cotton this year and enough to keep food on our table. Why do you ask?"

"I been thinking," said Joe Ray. "How 'bout we make a deal? Supposing I work in the cotton fields this year. How 'bout we split anything more than what last year's crop sold for." 20

Boss Bill could not believe what he was hearing.

"You work in the fields?" he stuttered. "Why, Joe Ray, you ain't worked in the cotton more than two hours in your whole life."

"I know," replied Joe Ray. "But, it's time I started pulling my weight around here, and besides, I need to get me some money. We got a deal, or not?"

"We got a deal, Son. And we're gonna start planting first thing Monday morning."

"That's fine with me," Joe Ray answered. "Now, I need to ask one more favor. Can I be gone next Friday?"

"Sure enough, boy," was his father's reply. "I know you been seeing Miss Charlene every Friday for months now. I also know after next week, she is going to be leaving. Mattie keeps me up on the goings-on around here. I been expecting old man McClanahan to find out about you all and run you off, but I guess you two been pretty lucky."

"Good. I won't miss another day after that," promised Joe Ray.

When he and his father finished their meal, he went out on the porch to ponder his decision. In a little while, Boss Bill joined him.

"If this weather holds, looks like you and Luther are going to have some good days for fishing," he commented.

"Yeah, and some better days for planting cotton," Joe Ray answered, smiling.

Chapter Four
Luther's Plan

It was almost noon when Luther rode his mule up to the front of Joe Ray's Shack. This was the time they planned to go fishing. Joe Ray took his usual place behind Luther on the mule and they were off. To Joe Ray, today was no different than any of the hundreds of other times he had gone fishing with Luther. Except today, he wasn't thinking about fishing. His mind was on what lay in his future.

It was near mid-afternoon by the time the two young men reached the bend of the river. Luther tied his mule to one of the sycamore trees to graze in the tall grass, and he and Joe Ray boarded the canoe. They always crossed the river when they arrived this early in the day because the larger trees on the far side provided a much cooler shade.

Joe Ray replaced his broken fishing pole from two days earlier with an old one he discarded a few months before. The sun was boiling down upon the river and the fish were biting really slow, so Joe Ray and Luther just lounged on the bank and waited for the cooler part of the evening.

"Ever been to Macon?" Luther asked, as he pulled himself up from the grassy spot where he was lying under one of the sycamore trees.

"Yeah, once a long time ago. Boss Bill took me and my mother with him when he went to a cotton growers' meeting. But, that was before the war and I can't remember even being there. Why do you want to know if I been to Macon for, Luther?"

"I wuz jus' thinkin', Joe Ray. Wouldn't hit be nice iffen we could take us a trip all de way up yonder to Macon? I ain't never been more'n fifty miles away frum heah in my whole lifetime. I been talkin' to some of de other black folks dat come by de plantation on their way to Macon.

Dey's been tellin' me dat up there, dey have places where us Negro folks can git together an' have us a good time like dem white folks do. Why don' we go to Macon, Joe Ray? We ain't never goin' to be no better off'n we is right now, iffen we stay heah on dis ol' plantation farm. All we do is set 'round an' listen to de ol' folks talk 'bout how good life wuz afore the war, an' come down heah to dis ol' river fishin' or frog huntin' mos' ever day. Dat's got so it ain't much fun no more, 'cause like yo' know, de big'uns we hooks mos' always gits away. Let's do take us a trip to Macon, Joe Ray. What yo' say?"

"Now, how we going to get the money to take a trip to Macon, Luther? Me and you both together ain't got one greenback dollar bill. And how was you plannin' on us gettin' there, anyway?"

"Jus' say yo'll go wif me, Joe Ray. Jus' yo' say yo'll go an' I'll figure us out a way. Dem other Negro folks say dey got music playin', gamblin' wif cards, good lookin' young women folks, any color yo' want an' all the licker yo' wants to drank," Luther begged. "Jus' say yo'll go."

Joe Ray interrupted Luther and said, "Quit your dreamin' and put some more bait on your hook, Luther. It's 'bout time for the fish to start bitin'. Besides, we don't know anything 'bout music. We don't have any money for card playin'. I already got me the best lookin' woman in the whole state of Georgia, and neither one of us has ever drunk any hard liquor."

Both Joe Ray and Luther put a fresh bait of worms on their hooks and settled down a little closer to their fishing poles. The sun was going down and the water was beginning to cool, which usually caused the catfish to start moving around, looking for their supper.

Before another hour passed, the stillness of the late afternoon was broken by the low roar of the large iron wheels on the tracks that ran along the banks of the river. At first, all that could be heard was an almost silent roar far in the distance. The roar became louder and louder as the train came closer to where the two were fishing. Joe Ray and Luther were so familiar with the sound that they could count the number of cars in the train by the number of times the joint in the nearby rails screeched. The Macon to Atlanta was right on schedule today. As usual, you could set your

25

clock by her.

It seemed that each evening, the passing of the train woke up all the creatures in the river. Before she was out of sight, every frog along the muddy banks began to croak and the catfish began to stir. But today, when the train was gone, the fish were not the only thing that began to stir.

"Dat's how we'll git toMacon," Luther shouted, jumping to his feet as if he were ready to leave immediately. "We'll ride de train."

"Ride the train? Where we going to get money to ride the train?" Joe Ray wanted to know. "We ain't hardly got enough money to ride your ol' mule, and that don't cost a thing."

"I'll figger hit out," Luther mumbled under his breath. "I'll figger out how to git de money fo' us to go to Macon, yo' jus' wait an' see."

Joe Ray and Luther stayed on the banks of the river until the soft glow of daylight began to turn into gray dusk, but they talked very little. They were meditating on two separate sets of ideas. Joe Ray was thinking about how he was going to be able to work and earn enough money so he could have a life with Charlene, while Luther was thinking about how he could get enough money to get himself and Joe Ray to Macon without having to work.

"I might just as well tell you," Joe Ray said to his companion as the two left the river. "From now on, I don't think I'm going to have time to do much fishin'.

"How come?' Luther asked.

"Because, from now on, I'll be helping Boss Bill and

26

the others in the cotton."

"Yo' gone slap dab crazy?" Luther questioned.

"Yo' must have lost all de knowin's yo' ever had iffen yo' druther give up layin' 'round in de shade fishin' to go out in de boilin' sun to work in de cotton."

Joe Ray ignored Luther's comments and began telling him about his plans to earn enough money so he could marry Charlene.

"Now, I know yo' crazy," Luther stated, throwing back his head as he let out a loud roar of laughter. "Do yo' think fo' one split second ol' man 'Clanahan gonna let his little Miss Charlene marry up wif de likes of yo'? Yo' need to get 'em crazy notions outta yo' head an' start helpin' me figger out us a way to git up to Macon. Anyhow, I done tol' yo' dey got plenty of good lookers in de city. We could go up there an' have us a good ol' time an' yo' little sweetie wouldn't never know nuttin' 'bout it, as iffen she cared."

By the time they reached the row of shacks, Luther determined he was going to be unable to change Joe Ray's mind and he was becoming more upset. He wasn't worried as much about Joe Ray as he was the fear of having to join the others in the cotton fields. The only way to get Joe Ray's mind off that Miss Charlene, Luther decided, was to figure our some way to get him to Macon. He had no idea of how he was going to get the money, but he was sure of one thing; he was going to find a way.

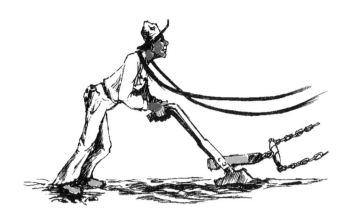

Chapter Five
Life In The Cotton Fields

Soon after daybreak on Monday morning, the cotton fields on the Franklin plantation came alive. Everyone's livelihood depended on the sale of their cotton, and Joe Ray, more than anyone, was anxious to get started.

News of his plans spread to the entire group, but few expected him to last out the first day. By sundown, all their doubts were dispelled, for he had worked harder than anyone in the fields. He was ahead of everyone the whole day and kept encouraging the others to keep up with his pace.

Luther, needless to say, did not show. He had not yet accepted the idea of his lifelong friend giving up a life of leisure to go to work.

As quitting time approached, Mattie and some of the other Negro women left the fields in order to prepare their evening meal. Sometime later, when the others came home to partake of the food the women prepared, they overheard Mattie issuing a strong reprimand to Luther.

"De Good Book say dat if yo' don' work, yo' don' eat," she was saying, as she reminded him of the size of his appetite.

Luther did not take suppper with the others that evening. Instead, he went off somewhere by himself, pouting at Joe Ray. He did, however, come to the fields the next morning, but it was not until long after the others went to work. Mattie's nagging did little more that add fuel to the flame of resentment Luther had toward Joe Ray, for anytime their work brought the two into close contact, Luther would say such things as, "I'd druther be a pore boy up in Macon, than to stay heah in de cotton fields an' git marryin' rich."

Joe Ray ignored him as best he could. He knew that if he were to make a success of his goal, he would need all the help he could get.

By the end of the third day, Joe Ray could not believe the condition of his body. He worked harder than he had ever done before in his life. His muscles were sore and his fingers ached, but he never entertained the thought of giving up. He talked the others into planting twice the amount of cotton they had the year before. This was no hard task, for everyone wanted to help him succeed. They knew life would be better for them if there was a good income from the sale of the cotton.

There had always been enough food, but the fear of when that might end, was enough to give everyone the energy they needed to produce. Whatever food could not be grown on the plantation had to be purchased in Dublin, and the money from the sale of a good cotton crop would be more than sufficient to do so.

On Thursday morning, Joe Ray was the first one in the fields. He had been working for some time before the others arrived.

"Yo' works like a man possessed," Mattie commented when she learned how long Joe Ray had been at work.

This was true, he had to admit, but his drive gave energy to the others. More cotton was planted in the previous three days than would have been in two weeks in years past.

"Just get through the day," Joe Ray kept telling himself. "Tomorrow, you can see Charlene." This thought made him work with such zeal that the others could not keep up. By evening, he was exhausted, but he was uplifted by his thoughts of the coming day.

After supper that evening, Joe Ray and his father relaxed on the porch, listening to the sounds of the kneedeepers from a nearby pond. A whipporwill perched in one of the oak trees up on the rise near their once beautiful mansion, was answering the call of another, somewhere in the distance. A breeze began to blow out of the north, making the cool of the evening much more pleasant.

The Negro men did not gather at the Franklin shack this evening, and Joe Ray was glad. He needed, for the first time in his life to seek the advice of his father. During his entire eighteen years, he had taken Boss Bill for granted. Only now, could he realize what it must be like for his father. No wonder, Joe Ray thought, he looks older than his sixty-two years. Within the last decade, his father had lost his wife, all but a mere handful of his Negro workers, which once numbered over a hundred, and his former plantation was no larger than that of a share-cropper's farm.

The thought of Charlene being gone for so long, made Joe Ray realize what it must be like to have all of one's dreams come tumbling down around him.

As he sat in silence on the porch of this run-down shack, watching the moon rise slowly behind the remains of their once elaborate plantation home, he was overcome by the pity he felt for his father. For the first time, he realized the great toll the war had taken on all of their lives. How wonderful it would be, he thought, if their plantation home and acreage were still intact. Then, he would have something to offer Charlene, and his mother might even still be alive.

"How much would it cost to restore our home?" he asked Boss Bill, breaking the silence.

His father sat for some time, pondering the question. "I guess more than either of us will ever possess," was his reply.

"And how much is that?" Joe Ray persisted.

Boss Bill began to stare up toward the deserted remains. "I guess about five thousand dollars by now," was his somewhat conservative estimate. "It would not have been so much right after the burning," he said. "But now, I'm sure it would take at least that amount."

"Then, we got to find a way," Joe Ray insisted, with so much enthusiasm, Boss Bill began to smile.

"I ain't never seen such a change in a boy before in all my born days," he said. "All of a sudden you are doing more in the cotton fields than any other three of us put together, and now, you're talking about fixing up that old mansion. What's come over you, anyway? It couldn't have anything to do with your pretty little Miss Charlene, could it?"

Joe Ray began to confide in his father like he had never done before. He explained how he felt about Charlene, and how much he wanted to marry her. He also told Boss Bill of his fear of losing her to some wealthy plantationeer, or even worse, to some northerner, once she was in Atlanta.

"If I could only restore our home," he explained, "at least I would have something to offer her."

Boss Bill sensed the urgency in his son. He was astounded by the hidden ambition he saw beginning to surface. He could also begin to feel the warmth of a flame starting to burn within himself. Maybe, he thought, Joe Ray's dreams were adding the fuel he needed to rekindle his own fire. Maybe, after all these years, someone else shared his yearning for restoration. The idea of living in the mansion again, brought new life to Boss Bill, but he did not want to instill any false hope in his son.

"It would be a painstaking task," Boss Bill began to speak, "but I believe there is a way it could be done."

Joe Ray got up from where he was sitting and moved closer to his father. "Tell me how," he said in a voice that was almost pleading.

"Well, you see, Son," Boss Bill said. "Ever since the

33

war, the factory owners up north have been trying to buy as much southern property as they can. They began purchasing lands in the Carolinas almost as soon as the war ended. Now, they are trying to buy land right here in our own area. I hear anyone who still owns land in Georgia can easily get a loan from the banks. The bankers know if they have to foreclose, their interests will be protected because the northerners will buy up the land at top prices when it goes to auction.

As you know, Joe Ray, we don't have much land left, but what we have got is ours, free and clear. Maybe we could get a loan from the bank to restore the mansion. But, if we do, you have to understand, we take a chance on losing it all."

Not knowing anything about business matters, Joe Ray asked, "If we get money from the bank, how we going to pay it back?"

"We would have to repay the loan with the money we get from the sale of the cotton," his father replied.

"Can we do that?" Joe Ray wanted to know.

"Only if we plant in all the land we have, even the fields that have been allowed to lay idle."

"Then, we can do it," Joe Ray insisted with a gleam in his eye. "Then, we can do it."

Joe Ray and his father sat on the porch until almost midnight. They were both filled with excitement as they discussed their plans. First, they would finish planting the cotton. Boss Bill decided he would spend all that he had in order to seed as much of the land as was possible. He knew, at the present pace, all would be lost anyway. After all, he thought, he now had a partner. Joe Ray had finally become the son he always wanted.

At last, Boss Bill stood up. He stepped off the porch onto the hard clay they called their yard. Joe Ray joined him a moment later. As they stood side-by-side looking up the rise toward the half-burned mansion, Boss Bill laid his arm on Joe Ray's shoulder.

"Have faith, my son," he said, "the South may rise again."

Chapter Six
Farewell To Charlene

As Joe Ray bathed the next morning, he did not hang the burlap sacks around the tub, for there was no need. It was not light enough for anyone to see. There was no need to be up so early, but he could not wait to meet the day. He had to share his plan with Charlene.

By the time he finished grooming, Boss Bill was also out of bed. Their enthusiastic conversation of the night before resumed as if neither had ever slept. They talked non-stop about their plans until the others came by their shack, on the way to the fields.

After everyone was gone, Joe Ray made his way up to the half-charred remains of what was once their home. He opened one of the two doors that led to the large entrance hall. There, before him, lay a large mound of blackened rubble. Pieces of half-burned furniture lay on the staircase that led from the ground floor to the sleeping quarters upstairs.

All of the walls and ceilings were black from smoke and the extreme heat that once engulfed the beautiful home. He made his way across the massive pile of destruction and began climbing the stairway leading to the west wing. As he opened the door to one of the enormous guest rooms, he was surprised to find it had been spared much of the devestation. As he examined room after room, Joe Ray was pleasantly surprised at his findings. Much of this wing suffered only smoke damage, unlike the other portion of the home, which was almost totally destroyed.

Joe Ray had not been inside the dwelling for many years, nor had he reason to be. Immediately after the fire, he moved into one of the slave shacks with his mother and Boss Bill.

His parents intended to rebuild the mansion at once, but his mother became very ill shortly thereafter, and within two months, she was dead. Joe Ray never heard his father discuss restoring the house after that.

As he stood in awe of the large job that lay before him, he suddenly became stunned with the fear of his inabilities. But, he knew what he lacked in knowledge, he would be able to make up in hard work. Anyway, he knew Boss Bill possessed all the skills needed to get the job done. He did not have time to dwell on this matter, now. It was time to leave, if he was going to see Charlene.

He barely reached the grove, when he saw the buggy carrying Sara and Charlene come into view. As they approached the storage buildings, Joe Ray realized something was wrong. Sara did not turn her buggy as she had always done. Today, she drove the buggy up close, in front of one of the buildings, as if to hide it from view.

"I was almost not able to come today," explained Charlene, as Joe Ray helped her down from the buggy.

"My father and mother are not making the regular Friday trip to Macon because I have to leave for Atlanta on Monday. He postponed their trip until then. We owe this meeting to Sara's craftiness. She insisted on taking me for a ride over our plantation one last time before I departed. She must stay here with us for fear she might be seen by some of the others if she leaves.

We knew we were taking a chance by coming here, but I cannot leave without seeing you one more time. Forgive me, Joe Ray, but I cannot tarry long. I just came to tell you how much I'll miss you and that I'll write to you as often as I can."

"Yo' mus' hurry," interrupted Sara. "We will have to go soon. I don't know de whereabouts of yo' father, an' yo' know it would not be good if we's found out."

"A lot has happened," Joe Ray began to speak, completely ignoring Sara's insistance to leave. "Boss Bill and I are going to restore the mansion. We are going to begin work on it as soon as our cotton is planted. Don't you see, Charlene, at last, I'll be able to ask you to marry me and furnish you a place to live equal to what you are accustomed."

"We mus' go!" insisted Sara again as she reached out

to help Charlene back onboard.

"I will marry you," Charlene said to Joe Ray, as he helped her back ito the buggy. "I would marry you now, if I could. But, since I'm not yet old enough, I must go to Atlanta to satisfy the wishes of my father. I am anxious to hear about your plans to restore your mansion, but you will have to tell me all about it in your letters. We must go."

Charlene leaned forward to give Joe Ray one last goodby kiss, then suddenly hesitated and grew grossly pale. Joe Ray turned to see what had startled her and found himself standing face-to-face with Charlene's father. None of them knew how long he had been hiding, but it didn't matter. He had heard enough to make him furious.

"No daughter of mine will ever marry the likes of you," he yelled at Joe Ray. "Not as long as I'm alive. And as for your mansion, you might as well quit dreaming. That worthless father of yours does not even have what it takes to rebuild the shack you live in. And as for you, Charlene, I forbid you to ever see this no-good boy again. I guess I need not ask how long these meetings have been going on. I know the three of you would lie to me, and I've had all I can endure for one day. Follow me back to where you belong," he growled at Sara, "and rest assured, I will deal with you later."

John McClanahan went back to one of the buildings where he had been hiding. He led his saddle horse to the outside and as he mounted , he said to Joe Ray, "It's only a matter of time until I buy the remainder of your father's holdings, and I can take pleasure in not having to see any of you Franklins ever again."

Joe Ray stood dumbfounded as he watched Charlene's father ride off with the buggy close behind. He thought of a hundred things he would like to have said, but remained silent instead. He was afraid of what any outburst from him would do to his relationship with Charlene.

As soon as they were out of sight, Joe Ray walked away. He did not head in the direction of their own plantation, however. Instead, he headed toward the bend in the river. He needed some time alone to sort out the happenings of the past few minutes.

As he walked toward the river, he began to question the need for restoration of their plantation home. He knew that Charlene's father would do anything he could to keep them apart. Now that she was leaving for Atlanta, this would not be difficult for him. Joe Ray would not give up easily. He knew somehow, he would find a way.

He needed time alone to work out what he would do. At this moment, he was so filled with so much hatred toward Charlene's father, that he could not sort out his own thoughts. He never before realized how cruel life could be. Just a few days before, he was living a carefree life, bumming around with Luther, and looking forward to nothing more than his weekly visits with Charlene. And now, just a fortnight later, he found himself in a state of frustration.

As he approached the bend in the river, he found the one thing he least needed. Seated in the tall grass, leaning back against on of the sycamore trees, was Luther. He would like to have gotten away before he was seen, but like everything else that had happened to him today, there was no such luck.

"Where's yo're fishin' pole?" Luther wanted to know as he saw Joe Ray approaching, "an' I need some bait. I'se all outta worms."

"I don't have a pole, and I didn't come to fish," exclaimed Joe Ray. "I came to do some serious thinking."

"What's so serious yo' got to think 'bout?" Luther asked.

Joe Ray spent the next half-hour explaining to Luther his feelings for Charlene and what happened earlier in the day. Luther listened to what he had to say without interruption.

When he finished, Luther looked him straight in the eye and asked, "When we goin' to Macon, Joe Ray? I 'spose we won' be goin' now, 'til yo' sell dat big cotton crop."

"What's wrong with you, Luther?" Joe Ray asked in a not too kind voice. "Don't you ever think about anybody but yourself?"

"I'se thinkin' 'bout both of us," Luther replied. "I thought both of us wuz goin' to Macon. Yo' said we wuz, as soon as I can figger out a way to git de money."

"No, you said we were," came his companion's sharp reply. "You said you were going to find a way to ride that dadburn train, but I didn't say I was going with you."

"But yo' will, quick as I git de money, won' yo'? Luther pleaded. "I don' know nuttin 'bout city ways an' yo' been to Macon before, so yo' could watch out after me. 'Sides, yo' know good as I do, yo' ain't never gonna marry

42

up wif dat Miss Charlene. Her ol' man ain't never gonna heah to none of dat."

"Yes, I will marry her, you just wait and see," Joe Ray snapped. "When I sell our cotton and she gets back from Atlanta, I'm sure going to marry her, and I could care less about what her pappy wants."

"But, iffen yo' do go 'head an' marry her, we ain't never gonna be able to go up to Macon," Luther growled, as Joe Ray started to walk away.

"I've got to get away from here," Joe Ray decided. He could not think and listen to Luther rave on about Macon at the same time. He had gone no further than where Luther tied up his old mule, when he heard him yell.

"I let yo' know soon's I gits de money. Den, we can start plannin' on leavin'," Luther was bellowing. "We can go up to Macon an' have oursefs a good time while Miss Charlene is in 'Lanta an' she won't never know nuttin' a'tall 'bout it. Say yo'll go soon as I git some cash, Joe Ray."

"Hell, yeah, I'll go to Macon with you when you get the money, if I ain't too old to travel," he said mockingly.

Joe Ray turned and out of sheer frustration, started to move on, slapping Luther's mule a sharp blow on his hinder parts. Next thing he knew, he was picking himself up off the ground. The mule let him have it with both feet, sending him clear up onto the railroad tracks. Seeing what happened, Luther broke into a fit of laughter.

"Damn you, Luther," Joe Ray screamed, "you and that old mule are just exactly alike. Both of you are just as hardheaded as a goat."

43

With that, Joe Ray began the three-mile walk home. Might just as well get back to working the cotton, he decided. Everything else he'd done all day had gotten him into trouble.

Joe Ray made his way back home and changed into his working clothes. Soon, he was in the fields with the others. He worked at some distance, however, because he wanted to avoid any conversation. He needed time to work himself out a game plan.

He labored through the remaining hours of the day, barely conscious of what he was doing. He wrestled with himself about what he should do in order to be able to marry Charlene. No sooner would he come up with an idea, than some reason came to mind why his idea wouldn't work. And most every reason was due to the lack of money.

Joe Ray worked feverishly through the rest of the day to ward off the hypertension caused by his anger toward Charlene's father. The other hands were leaving the fields before he realized where the time had gone. He did not work on after the others quit, which was customary for him. Today, his energy was drained. Not from the work he had done, but from the nerve-wracking happenings with old man McClanahan and Luther. And he was also getting sore as the result of the revenge of Luther's mule.

After supper that evening, Joe Ray shared the happenings of the day with his father, especially the part about Charlene's father wanting to buy the remaining part of their plantation.

Boss Bill listened to what his son had to say. Then,

without a word, he got up out of his chair and disappeared into the shack. Joe Ray could tell by the noise of furniture being moved that his father was searching for something. In a little while, Boss Bill emerged with writing paper and pencil in hand. Still, without uttering a word, he beckoned to Joe Ray to follow him. The two made their way up the rise where the remains of the mansion was located.

"Write down what I tell you," Boss Bill said in a voice that seemed somewhat commanding. "Old man McClanahan got some notion that he's going to buy us out, does he?"

His father continued. "Well, we'll just see about that. I think it's about time we stopped selling and started doing some buying ourselves."

"Write down what I tell you," he repeated as he extracted a wooden folding rule from his pocket. "Let's see now, we need four thousand feet of this and eight hundred board feet of that, a hundred pounds of nails and ten buckets of paint, ten window panes this size and three more of that size."

Boss Bill was rattling off a list of materials almost faster than Joe Ray could write. Joe Ray knew nothing of what would be needed to put the mansion back into it's original state, but he was sure pleased at the renewed interest Boss Bill was showing.

"We'll sell no more," his father stated, as he folded his rule and started back to the shack. "I always thought your mother and I would grow old in the mansion, and when we were gone, you would carry on. But, when the mansion burned, and then, your mother died, I just gave up."

"Now that you are grown and have some dreams of your own, we will begin again. We may lose everything we have to the bank, but we will not sell another morsel of our land. As soon as the cotton is planted, we will do whatever is necessary to start rebuilding," said his father.

When they reached the shack, they found the day offered yet another surprise. There on the porch sat Sara. Seated on each side of her, were her two boys. A small bundle of clothing lay at her feet.

"Mr. John done told us we had to leave his place," she began to sob. "An' we ain't got nowhere else we can go. I ain't got no family dat can help us, neither, 'ceptin' one sister, an' I don' even know iffen she is still livin'. Her an' her man wuz both sold off 'afore de war, an' last I heard, dey was somewhere way up in de Carolinas. I guess dey probably both dead by now.

Sara continued, "Mr. John got so mad 'cause he found out 'bout me helpin' Miss Charlene to see yo', Mr. Joe Ray, dat he told me an' my young'uns to git offin his place, an' dat he hoped he didn't never have to look at us again. Do yo' reckon we could live heah wif yo' all? We would work hard to earn our keep an' we wouldn't be no bother, neither."

Joe Ray looked questioningly at his father. Boss Bill nodded approvingly and then, disappeared inside.

"For as long as you want to stay," Joe Ray assured her, placing his arm around her shoulder. "Take your choice of any of the shacks for tonight, and we will make other arrangements in the morning."

46

"I'm sorry," he went on, "this is all my fault, but you can be sure that someday, I'll make it up to you."

When Joe Ray finished making Sara and her children as comfortable as possible on such short notice, he made his way back to his own shack and fell into bed. What a day this has been, he thought, as he stretched his tired frame upon his cot.

Just before he fell asleep, he heard his father say from the other side of the room, "Good night, Son. Today, I think you became a man."

The next several weeks were torture. Two months passed with no word from Atlanta. Joe Ray kept himself busy with the mounting chores on the plantation, but he could not keep his mind off Charlene. Why had she not written? Surely, he thought, she could not have forgotten about him so quickly. Maybe she was afraid of what her father would do if he found out. That's nonsense, he decided. They both knew her father did not approve, but that never stopped them before.

"Stop making excuses for her," he said to himself. "There is some good reason why she has not written. I just have to find out what it is."

Anyway, in three weeks, he would be nineteen, and he was sure Charlene would not let that occasion pass without some correspondence.

A lot had taken place since Charlene departed. Every square foot of available soil was planted in cotton. Everyone on the place seemed anxious to help Joe Ray fulfill his dream.

47

In addition, the added help he received from Sara and her boys did much to add to the productivity. Since coming to the plantation, the three had pulled more than their share of the load. Everyone worked with more enthusiasm than Joe Ray ever saw them do before.

Even Luther joined in now and then to lend a helping hand. Joe Ray did not know if this was due to Mattie's constant nagging, or if he just came around to rib him about Charlene. Whatever the case, it did not matter to Joe Ray. He was willing to listen to Luther's snide remarks in exchange for the work he provided.

Luther had not given up on their trip to Macon, however. Every Friday, he would take off from work and go fishing. Each time, he would return with renewed interest in making the trip. Joe Ray thought it must be because of the train to Macon. It ran by the river where Luther was fishing and he thought this was what renewed his excitement. Whatever it was, Luther always came home with more encouragement for Joe Ray to go with him.

"Yo' ain't never gonna heah no more frum Miss Charlene," he would say. "She done went up there to de big city an' found herself 'nother beau. Yo' might as well make up yo' mind to dat fact an' start havin' yoursef some fun. Anyhow, quick as I gits me some money, we gonna leave."

Joe Ray ignored Luther's comments. He was right about one thing, though, he had to admit. It had been a long time since he had done anything just for fun. He worked from sunup to sundown day after day. The only break in his

48

routine was his weekly Saturday morning visit to the post office in Dublin. He had made this trip every Saturday morning since Charlene's departure, hoping each time, that there might be some word.

When she first left, Joe Ray would saddle up and be gone before anyone else was out of bed. But now, he was later and later getting started. It was the disappointment of not ever getting a letter that haunted him. So, every week, he rode back to the plantation a little more frustrated. Even on his birthday, there had been no word.

He would write to her if only he knew where to write, but there was no way for him to find out her whereabouts. Mattie inquired from the Negro folks at the McClanahan place every Sunday when she went to church. But, John McClanahan went to great lengths not to let any of them know, for fear the information might be passed on to Joe Ray.

There was so much he needed to share with her. He wanted to let her know about the progress they had made in the planting of the cotton, and the money he anticipated it would bring. But, most of all, he wanted to tell her about the restoration of the mansion.

The restoring of the mansion went much faster than Joe Ray ever dreamed it would. As soon as the cotton planting was completed, he and Boss Bill went to Dublin ans secured the loan they needed from the bank. Already, the charred timbers and the half-burned furniture was hauled away. The walls were already scrubbed and the tattered, weather-beaten drapes discarded. And too, the smell of smoke had been replaced by the sweet aroma of pine, which emerged from the stacks of new lumber already delivered.

Joe Ray was delighted that he and Boss Bill had not done all the work. Everyone on the plantation pitched in to help, as if the dwelling were to be their own. The Negores seemed to be happier working on the mansion than they did loafing as they had done in years past.

But, this made Joe Ray uncomfortable. The tending of the cotton was everyone's responsibility because their livelihood depended upon it. But, there was no obligation for them to work on the mansion. They all understood from the beginning that they would receive no pay, but that didn't hamper their willingness to work. Joe Ray's dream had become their own.

By the time the cotton needed hoeing the first time, all the new framing was completed and much of the inside work started. But now, the building project had to be put aside. The cotton fields must come first. After all, without the money from the sale of the cotton, the loan could not be paid and all would be lost. The plantation would be sold.

"This loan must be paid in full," the banker had told them. "And there will be no extensions. If the loan is not paid at the time of the sale of your cotton, we will foreclose."

Several days after their loan was completed, Joe Ray learned that John McClanahan was on the bank's board of directors. If he and his father defaulted in payment, McClanahan would be among the first to know, and he would not fail to seize the opportunity to buy up what was left of their plantation.

50

Chapter Seven
Luther Goes To Macon

"Git up, Joe Ray. We gotta git goin'," came a voice from outside Joe Ray's window. Joe Ray opened his eyes to discover it was still pitch black. He knew it was not yet daylight and thought he was dreaming.

"Git up, Joe Ray, we gotta git goin'," came the voice again, and Joe Ray realized it was Luther.

Joe Ray pulled himself from his cot and opened the door to the shack. When he did, he saw Luther standing at the edge of their front porch. It was still so dark that Joe Ray could see nothing but Luther's outline in the soft glow of the remaining moonlight.

"What you doing up at this time of night, Luther?" Joe Ray wanted to know. "It ain't even daylight yet, and we don't have to catch that train till late afternoon."

"I know," replied Luther, "but we got to git a early

51

start. We gotta lot to do 'fore we git oursefs ready to leave. Ma Mattie is already fixin' us some ham biskits to take wif us an' I done tol' Pa to go 'head an' be hitchin' up de horse to de buggy, so he be ready to take us down to de station."

"Hell, what you do that for, Luther? We going to catch the train this afternoon, not the one that ran yesterday. It ain't much more than left Macon on the way to Savannah yet. Why don't you go back to your shack and I'll let you know when I'm ready to go." With that, Joe Ray reentered the shack and slammed the door, leaving Luther standing on the porch.

Joe Ray was as anxious to get started as Luther, and the anxiety of their trip had kept him awake far past midnight. He fell back on his cot, hoping to sleep until at least midmorning. He lay on his bed until the early morning light began to creep through the tiny windows on each end of their shack, but more sleep did not come.

His plans were to leave Luther in Macon and go from there to Atlanta alone. He had not yet found a way to break the news to Luther because he knew Luther would not be happy, being left in Macon by himself.

He did not know how, but he knew he wasn't going to give up until he located Charlene, yet, he was afraid of what he might find. Would she be glad to see him, or would she have found someone else? Whatever the case, he had to know. He could not bear the frustration any longer.

Although Joe Ray was as excited about their journey as Luther, he could better hide his anxiety. This, he knew, was due to his fear of making the trip. After all, he had no experience of city life. His father did his best to prepare him for what to expect, but so much had happened since Boss Bill had been to Atlanta.

The entire city was burned during the war, as well as he could remember. The southern skies were red for days and the air was filled with the smell of smoke so strong, it burned his nostrils as it was carried onto their plantation by breezes from the north.

Since the war, though, the rumor was that Atlanta had been rebuilt to a size larger than it was before the burning. But, Joe Ray did not care, because his desire to find Charlene outweighed his fear of the city.

Luther, on the other hand, had no fear at all. He was planning on Joe Ray being with him all the time, and besides,Macon was much smaller than Atlanta, so he would be alright.

"What am I worrying about Luther for?' Joe Ray thought. "After all, he will probably steal the key to the city before he leaves, anyhow."

Movement on the far side of the room told Joe Ray that Boss Bill was awake.

"What you doing up so early?" he asked his father. "It's too early for even you to be awake."

"Heck, I been awake ever since Luther started bellowing outside your window. I told Ole Ben when that young'un was born, he ought to drown him in the Oconee River. And this morning, I wished he had. First time I ever saw him, he kept staring at my watch chain, but it wasn't until he was six years old that he stole my watch. Ole Ben caught him and brought it back after giving him a good licking, but I know he was planning on stealing that watch ever since the day he was born. That's the sorriest black boy I ever seen. I sure wish he wasn't going with you."

"Don't worry, Daddy," Joe Ray replied. "He ain't going to cause me no trouble. Besides, he don't even know that I'm going on to Atlanta and I don't think I'll tell him until we get to Macon."

"Just the same, you keep an eye on that thieving black soul. I don't want him getting you in no kind of mischief. You been working too hard for the last few months and you need a rest. So, don't let Luther drag you all around Macon two or three days before you go on to Atlanta."

Boss Bill was sure right about working hard, Joe Ray thought. He had worked harder since early spring than all the rest of his life put together. Since the first sod was turned in mid-March, the labor had been endless. First, there was the plowing, which utilized the strength of every man and horse brute on the plantation.

Then came the planting of the cotton seed and after that, the hoeing. The cotton always needed hoeing. The much needed rain came, the cotton flourished, and so did the weeds. Day after day, Joe Ray and the five other men, not counting Boss Bill and Ole Ben, loosened the soil between the rows with the three-footed plows pulled by a single horse. Every other able-bodied person followed the plows with hoes, chopping the weeds from each of the cotton plants.

If the weeds were allowed to grow, they soon took over the cotton plants and would smother them out. Joe

Ray didn't allow that to happen. Even though he was tired from his labors, he had produced a first-rate crop. He was even spared the plague of the boll weavil.

Now, he decided, he could relax and spend some time enjoying the fruits of his labor. The cotton was all harvested and ready to be shipped to Savannah the following week for sale. The restoration of the mansion was within a week of completion, and now, it was time to relax.

"See you in about a week," he said to Boss Bill as he left the shack, "and thanks for everything."

'Everything' meaning the sixty-seven dollars Joe Ray tucked away in his coat pocket. His father gave him every last penny they had left.

"You're welcome, Son," came Boss Bill's reply. "But mind you, watch the departing of every cent. I hear Atlanta is full of people down from the north and they're out to get everything they can, whether by hook or crook. And don't let Luther know how much you got, either. Else, he'll have it stole from you before you even buy a train ticket."

"I'll be careful, Daddy," answered Joe Ray. "And I promise, I won't let Luther steal more stuff in Macon than he can haul back on the train." He laughed and strolled off toward Luther's shack.

As soon as Luther saw Joe Ray coming, he started yelling for Ole Ben to hurry up. "Come on, Pa," he yelled. "Let's go 'fore Joe Ray changes his mind."

By the time Joe Ray reached their shack, both, Ole Ben and Luther were in the buggy. He threw his grip which contained practically every stitch of clothing he owned, in

the back seat beside Luther and seated himself up front with
Ole Ben.

"I knows we're early," Ole Ben said to Joe Ray as
the buggy started moving. "But, I'm shore glad yo' come
on. I don' think I could put up wif dat boy much longer. He
more 'cited 'bout goin' to Macon than he is "bout goin' to
Hev'n."

"I don't think he's got to worry a lot about going to
Heaven, Ole Ben. I hear the Lord's got everything up there,
just like He wants it, and I'm sure He don't want Luther up
there carrying everything off."

"You probably right, Joe Ray." Ole Ben grinned and
tapped the horse on the hind parts to increase their pace.
"Yo' probably right."

On their way to the train station, Joe Ray and Ole
Ben talked about the happenings of the last few months.
Joe Ray was really grateful to him and Mattie for all they
had done to help himself and Boss Bill and he let him know
that as soon as the cotton was sold, they, along with the other
Negroes, would be rewarded.

Ole Ben reminded him that both, he and Mattie, were
getting old and assurance of being able to live out the remainder of their lives on the plantation was reward enough.

"Not enough," Joe Ray interrupted. "As long as me
and Boss Bill have a plantation, you and Mattie will be a
part of it."

"Yo' done growed up to be a fine man, Mr. Joe Ray,"
Ole Ben stated as he pulled the buggy along in front of the
train station platform. "Yessir, yo' a fine man, jus' like dat

daddy of your'n. Does yo' wan' me to wait fo' de train to come 'fore I leave?"

Joe Ray assured Ole Ben there was no need for him to wait until the train arrived.

"Whatever yo' say, Mr. Joe Ray," Ole Ben replied. "Yo' have yo'sef a whoppin' good time an' I be right here to pick yo' up nex' Sat'day when yo' gits back. An' Luther, yo' see to it that yo' don't come draggin' nothin' back home dat don't rightly belong to yo'."

When Ole Ben was out of sight, the two travelers made their way into the small station, which served as the Dublin Post Office. They strolled up to the ticket window, where the agent was sorting some mail.

"How much for a ticket to Atlanta, uhh, I need a ticket to Macon," Joe Ray inquired.

"Two dollars to Macon, six bits more on to Atlanta," the agent informed him.

"Then, I need a ticket to Macon," Joe Ray said.

Me, too," Luther interjected, extracting two one-dollar bills from the bib pocket of his overalls. "What time do de train git to Macon, anyway?" he asked the agent.

"'Bout dark," the agent informed, reaching a ticket to each of them.

"Now, what are we going to do for the next two hours?" Joe Ray asked Luther.

"I don' know, but one thing fer shore, we heah early 'nough so we won' miss de train," Luther replied.

"You sure enough right about that," Joe Ray said as the two boys went outside and seated themselves on the edge of the station platform, letting their feet dangle over the edge.

"How much money yo' got on yo'?" Luther asked.

"Not much," Joe Ray replied. "How about you?"

"I got twenty-two dollars left after I bought my ticket," was Luther's quick reply.

"I ain't got much more than that, myself," Joe Ray volunteered. "So, we better be careful how we spend it. Where'd you get ahold of twenty-four dollars, anyhow?"

"I been savin' ever since we been talkin' 'bout goin' to Macon, Joe Ray. I saved ever last penny I could git, an' den Ma Mattie let me borry twenty dollars."

That figures, Joe Ray thought. Mattie had probably saved for years to get twenty dollars that she could call her own, and now, Luther had talked her out of it.

"How'd you persuade Mattie to loan you twenty dollars, Luther?" Joe Ray asked. "She knows you won't never be able to pay her back."

"Well, she didn't really let me borry it," Luther mumbled while stuffing one of Mattie's ham biscuits into his mouth. "But, I'll have it back nex' Sat'day an' she won' never know it's been off de place."

"Well, I'll be a ....! I ain't never! Luther, you're lower down than a snakes bottom side. Of all the low-down, thieving tricks you ever pulled, this one caps the stack."

Joe Ray was so furious, he jumped down from where they were sitting and started pacing back and forth on the end of the crossties protruding from beneath the rail nearest the station.

"What's ever going to become of you, Luther? he

58

asked. "How long do you think you can get away with lying and taking advantage of everybody you know? When you stole those vegetables from our garden and sold them, I thought you had gone as far down as any human being could go, but you done dropped six or eight notches since then. I'm sure glad you ain't going on to Atlanta with me."

"What yo' mean, yo' is goin' on to 'Lanta? Yo' goin' to leave me in Macon all by mysef whilst yo' go on to 'Lanta? What yo' goin' on up there fer anyhow, Joe Ray?"

"I'm going there to find Charlene, if you must know." came Joe Rays' sharp reply.

Joe Ray's answer caused Luther to panic.

"Please don't leave me all by mysef in Macon," Luther pleaded. "Yo' knows I don't know nuttin' 'bout city ways an' somethin' terrible might happen to me 'fore yo' gits back. What is I 'sposed to do whilst yo' gone, anyhow?"

"Hell, I don't care what you do," yelled Joe Ray. "Maybe you can steal the last crumbs from some poor widow's table and get yourself hung for all I give a damn.

I'm going on to Atlanta and that's all there is to say about it. You didn't think I was crazy enough to spend a whole week in Macon with you, did you, anyway? Did you, Luther?"

"Fair 'nough," Luther roared. "Yo' go on up there to 'Lanta an' find dat Miss Charlene an' make a big fool outta yo'sef. I'm gonna find me one of dem gamblin' houses in Macon I'se been hearin' 'bout an' win me some big money. Den, I'se gonna put Ma Mattie's money I borry'd back where

I got it, wif a dollar extry. Now, what yo' think of dat, Joe Ray Franklin?"

"You're all heart, Luther. I'm overwhelmed by your generosity."

"I know'd yo' would be," Luther said sensing Joe Ray was beginning to calm down. "Heah, yo' want dis last ham biskit? I'se gittin' full."

"You ought to be getting full," Joe Ray said. "You done eat twelve, just while you been sitting there."

The roar of the locomotive could be heard as it approached the station. The large billows of smoke and steam could be seen as it neared the platform, where it's only two passengers were waiting. The screech of the wheels braking against the rails and the escaping steam drowned Luther's voice, but Joe Ray could tell by the gestures he was making, that he was rushing him to get aboard.

"What's your all-fired hurry?" Joe Ray asked. "They still got to take on water and wood in order to have fuel for the rest of the trip."

"Dis train ain't goin' nowhere wifout me on it," Luther managed to say as he thrust his ticket toward the conductor, with one hand, while he crammed the last ham biscuit into his mouth with the other.

"You can't get in this car," the conductor explained to Luther. "All blacks got to ride in the next car back," he said, pointing to the baggage car near the end of the train.

"Dat's alright wif me," Luther said. "I don't care iffen I hast to ride up yonder on de top, holdin' on to de smokestack, long a I gits mysef to Macon. See yo' when

60

we gits to de city," he yelled to Joe Ray, as he threw himself into the car that the conductor pointed out to him.

Joe Ray found himself a seat near the rear of the coach and enjoyed the scenery passing before him. The countryside was beautiful, but much of the devastation of the war could still easily be seen. Some of the passing plantations were being rebuilt, but many more lay in ruin; their owners unable to afford the high cost of starting over.

Sometime within the first hour, Joe Ray fell asleep, weary from the last weeks of work. The other stops between Dublin and Macon did not awaken him. Sometime later, he was aroused by the voice of the conductor, reminding him that he had reached his destination.

As he stepped from the car, he was greeted by none other than Luther.

"Look heah," he called to Joe Ray, as he emerged from the train. Luther was waving a handful of dollar bills.

"You should'a rode back there wif me," he said. "I done won mysef nine dollars in a poker game."

"Who you been playin' poker with?" Joe Ray inquired.

"Dem other Negro folks dat rode back there in de black car," Luther replied. "Dey done invited me to a big poker game dey goin' to have over yonder on Third Street t'morrow night, wherever dat is. Somewhere dey calls, Luke's Place."

"You just can't wait to get took," Joe Ray responded.

"What yo' mean, git took?" Luther answered. "Dey's de ones dat got took. I done took 'em suckers fer nine dollars." 61

"Whatever you say, Luther," Joe Ray stated, disinterested in his winnings. "I'm going to find me a room for the night and a good meal. I'm starved."

"Me, too," Luther agreed. "Dem ham biskits didn't keep us filled up very long, did they?"

Joe Ray started to reply, but thought better of it.

"Les' go see iffen we can find Luke's Place," Luther urged. "Dem black folks said Luke's got good eat'ins an' rooms to let out fer however long yo' need 'em."

Since it was late in the evening and was beginning to get dark, and for a lack of any better idea, Joe Ray agreed.

They asked directions from one of the railroad employees and within minutes, they found Luke's Place. Luke's Place, which to Luther had already become famous, was located near the railroad tracks about ten blocks from the train station, and was populated almost entirely by Negroes.

Upon entering the establishiment, Joe Ray questioned his judgement in agreeing to come here. The large dining room was filled with cigar smoke, and people with whiskey glasses were everywhere. They found a vacant table near where a piano was being played, far louder than Joe Ray thought necessary. When they were seated, a huge black man appeared, wearing a bibbed apron which looked as if it was splattered with blood.

"I'm de cook, de waiter, de bouncer, an' de handy man," the black man stated. "What be yo' fancy? We got beef steaks, rare or well done. We got taters, baked or mashed an' we got whiskey, warm or hot."

"We'll have two of 'em beef steaks, well done, some

62

of 'em mashed taters, an' a large glass of whiskey," Luther blurted.

"Steaks, potatoes, and a cup of coffee for each of us," Joe Ray corrected, ignoring the disgusted look he was getting from Luther.

"You fellers looking fer a place to sleep?" the waiter asked when he returned with their order.

"Yes, sir," Joe Ray answered. "I got to get myself a good night's sleep 'cause I got to be leavin' for Atlanta first thing in the morning."

"Then, yo' got the right place. I got plenty rooms right up stairs. Two dollars fer one room, sleep as many as yo' can." Then, leaning a little closer as if he didn't want anyone else to hear, he added, "Poker games in the back room, an' if yo' needs anythin' else, jus' ax fer Big Luke. Das' me."

"Just a room, I think will be all," Joe Ray stated.

"Not fer me," Luther said, becoming more and more excited. "I'm stayin' right down heah an' winnin' me a pocket full of dat poker money I been heahin' 'bout."

"Den, yo' shore come to de right place, too," Big Luke encouraged. "Yo' can stay here 'til yo' win it all, is fine wif me."

After Joe Ray finished his steak, which he decided had been cremated instead of just well done, he suggested that both of them retire for the night.

"Not me," Luther said, looking around as if he were searching for some lost object. "Iffen I can find one of dem poker games Big Luke wuz talkin' 'bout, I'm gonna start winnin' me some of dat cash right now."

"Suit yourself," Joe Ray said. "I'm going to bed."

When Joe Ray entered their room, he found a small oil lamp on a table near the center of his quarters. Several straw-filled mattresses were piled against one wall, and there were no other furnishings of any kind. He had never stayed in a rented room before, but he found this place to be far less than he expected.

Before the night gave way to dawn, Joe Ray was glad he had been able to sleep on the train. The laughter and loud piano playing downstairs kept him from sleeping the entire night, not to mention the fact that the mattress, on which he was lying, had more lumps than the back of Luther's mule.

The noise ceased just about the crack of dawn. A few moments later, Luther came staggering into the room. Joe Ray could tell at first glance, he had been partaking of the spirits he saw flowing so freely the night before.

"Is it time to go to bed, already?" Luther asked, fumbling around the room. "Where's de bed, anyhow?" he asked, puzzled.

"I think some black feller I know, lost it in a poker game," Joe Ray answered. "There, pull up one of those loser's cots and have yourself some sweet dreams," he said, pointing to the pile of straw mattresses. "Better still, take mine. I've got to get up anyway, so I can be on that seven o'clock train to Atlanta."

"Alright wif me," Luther growled, flopping down on the make-shift bed Joe Ray had been using. "Won mysef twenty more dollars," he said, as Joe Ray picked up his grip and headed for the door.

"I don't care if you win everything in Macon. You better be at that train station next Saturday morning if you are planning on going back to Dublin with me," Joe Ray warned.

As he made his exit, he heard Luther mumble just before he started to snore, "I'll be there fer shore, Joe Ray. Yo' can count on me bein' there fer shore."

Chapter Eight
Joe Ray Finds Charlene

It was shortly past noon when the train from Macon pulled into the Atlanta depot. As he stepped from his coach, the warm rays of sunlight were welcomed as they engulfed Joe Ray's body. What a beautiful Sunday afternoon, he thought, wishing Charlene could share it with him. First things first, he decided. He had to get himself a room and he needed a bath. The smell of cigar smoke lingered on his clothing and even if he knew where to find Charlene at this moment, he would not have her see him in his present state.

"May I take you someplace?" he was asked by a neatly dressed man who was sitting in a carriage.

Joe Ray realized that the carriage must be one of the ones for hire that he often heard Boss Bill speak about.

"Yes," Joe Ray answered, "to any place that has a nice clean room."

"Anyone in particular, sir," the driver asked, "we have

lots of hotels and rooming houses here in Atlanta."

"Any one you choose," Joe Ray instructed, "just as long as it is clean and has a real bed."

"Very well, sir," the driver answered as the carriage began to move away from the station. "I can tell this must be your first time in Atlanta, so I will take you to one of the city's finest."

In a short while, the driver stopped the carriage in front of a large, beautiful white building bearing the sign, 'Magnolia Hotel.'

"Here you are, sir," the driver stated. "May I be of further service?"

"As a matter of fact, maybe you can," Joe Ray answered. "How well do you know the city?"

"As well as anyone here, I "spose," the driver answered. "I've been driving this carriage ever since they started rebuilding Atlanta."

"Then, pick me up right here at ten o'clock in the morning, please," Joe Ray instructed.

"Very well, sir, and today's fare will be fifty cents," the driver answered.

Joe Ray paid the driver and entered the hotel. At first glance, he decided the carriage driver was right. This must surely be one of Atlanta's finest. He secured lodging for the remainder of the week and proceeded to take his much needed bath. Most of the remainder of the evening was spent in window shopping for a new suit he intended to purchase before he tried to find Charlene.

Next day, Joe Ray was up early and was off to buy

the suit he had chosen the previous evening, which was displayed in one of the men's stores only a short distance from his hotel. He went back to his room and dressed, then went down to the front of the hotel where the carriage was waiting.

He explained his situation to the driver and instructed him to visit every finishing school in Atlanta until he found Charlene. The first three places he visited resulted in a fruitless search, but with each visit, Joe Ray's excitement grew stronger. He knew that each time he failed, his chances of finding Charlene were getting better. It was at the fourth school that his search ended. Upon entering the establishment, Joe Ray announced to the lady that he had come to visit Miss Charlene McClanahan.

"Why, certainly, sir. Miss McClanahan is one of our most prized pupils. Whom shall I tell her is calling?"

"Tell her it's . . .just tell her it is someone who has traveled a great distance to visit her." Joe Ray answered.

"If you wish, sir. Please wait and I will see if Miss McClanahan can see you now."

The refined lady to whom Joe Ray had been speaking, entered one of the rooms adjacent to the entrance foyer without closing the door behind her.

"Miss Charlene," he heard her say, "a young gentleman is here to see you."

"Who is it?" he heard Charlene ask.

"The gentleman did not say," the lady answered, "only that he has traveled a long distance to see you."

"I'm sure it must be one of my brothers," he heard

Charlene's voice again. "They never do anything without being mysterious about it. They are probably in Atlanta on business for my father and came by to check on my well-being. Wonder which one of them it is?" she said as she entered the foyer.

Upon seeing Joe Ray, Charlene came to a halt as quickly as if she had walked into a stone wall. She stood, staring at him for a full minute without being able to speak. Then, suddenly, she burst into tears. Not tears of joy, as Joe Ray expected, but tears of anger.

"Well, of all the nerve," she began to speak. "After all these months without any answer to even one of my letters, you have the gall to show up here unannounced and act as if you expected to be greeted with some kind of a parade. Well, you can just parade yourself right back to where you came from, Joe Ray Franklin. I don't think I ever want to see you again as long as I live."

Charlene ran from the foyer before Joe Ray had time to utter a single word.

"But, please, let me explain," he started to speak, but to no avail. She was out of sight before any words came out.

The lady to whom Joe Ray had spoken earlier reentered the foyer.

"I must ask you to leave at once, sir," she said. "We cannot have our young ladies upset."

"But I must talk with her," Joe Ray said, ignoring what the lady had just told him. "Please, may I leave a message?"

"Well, alright," the lady consented, "but make it short."

Joe Ray wrote a note as, best he could, and handed it to the lady who stood impatiently waiting.

"Please see that she gets this," he stated, as the lady took the note and left the room. "Oh, and please let her know that I am staying at the Magnolia Hotel on Peachtree Street."

Joe Ray was saddened, but he knew more could not be accomplished by staying any longer. He went back to the carriage and instructed the driver to return to Peachtree Street. Upon his arrival at the hotel, he went straight to his room, where he remained for the rest of the day. He didn't know what to do next. His only hope was that the lady would give Charlene the message he left and that she would believe what he had written.

As he sat thinking, he wondered what could have happened to her letters. Then, suddenly it came to him. John McClanahan must once again, be making good his promise. He must have intercepted her letters when they arrived at the post office in Dublin. After all, he knew how much influence John McClanahan had in that part of the country. He was friends with the bankers, the railroad officials, cotton buyers and all the merchants for miles around. So, why not the Postmaster, also.

Besides, he did make his weekly visits into Dublin, while on his way to Macon. If he were friends with the Postmaster, then he would have easy access to anyone's mail.

As he lay on his bed until mid-morning the following day, Joe Ray could think of nothing else except his love for Charlene and his hatred for her father. Was there no end to what McClanahan would do to keep Joe Ray from seeing his daughter?

"I am in a losing situation," he thought. "If I can somehow win back Charlene, her father's anger toward me will only grow worse, and on the other hand, if I do anything vengeful toward him, then I take the chance of losing Charlene. One step at a time," he decided. "All I can do now, is wait for a reply to my message."

For the next two days, Joe Ray did little more than walk the streets of Atlanta. Twice, he rented a carriage and returned to the school Charlene attended, hoping to get a chance to see her, but such was not the case. Time for him was running out. He had no choice but to leave Atlanta on the coming Saturday.

He had to be back in order to deliver his cotton to Dublin, for shipment to Savannah the following week. The wagons would have to make many trips from the plantation to the rail station in order for the cotton to be ready for the Tuesday morning scheduled shipment.

"Just as well," Joe Ray thought. He could no longer afford to stay in Atlanta. His funds were rapidly being depleted. What with the purchase of his train tickets, room and meals, having to buy a suit of clothing, and the fares for the carriage, he was almost dead broke. He had enough for passage back to Dublin, but very little more.

On Thursday, Joe Ray walked the cobblestone streets of Atlanta until late evening. He had to do something to keep his mind off the predicament in which he found himself. Besides, he did not possess the funds to do anything else. It was shortly after dark when he returned to the hotel and started up the stairs to his room.

"Only one more day in Atlanta," he thought, "and I must leave without even being able to talk to Charlene."

"Excuse me, sir. Are you Mr. Joe Ray Franklin?" the clerk behind the desk inquired of him.

"Yes, I am," was Joe Ray's reply.

"Then, I have a message for you, sir," the clerk said, reaching a letter to him.

Joe Ray sat down on the bottom step of the stairway leading up to his room. He opened the letter and began to read.

Dear Joe Ray,

I believe I may have acted hastily when you visited me on Monday. I have had time to reconsider, and would like very much to talk to you. If you can find it in your heart to forgive my rudeness, I will be looking forward to your return visit at ten o'clock tomorrow morning.

Cordially,
Charlene

Upon reading the letter, Joe Ray let out such a yell that it startled everyone in the hotel lobby.

"You must control yourself, sir. We have other

guests," the clerk said as Joe Ray bounded up the stairs, taking three steps at a time.

Joe Ray entered his room and threw himself upon his bed. He read the message from Charlene several times before he was overtaken by peaceful slumber.

He did not awaken until an hour after daylight the next morning. When he awoke and realized it was full light, he became alarmed that he might have overslept. He ran to the window and looked across the street at the large clock which was displayed on the courthouse dome. He was relieved to discover that he had more time than he needed.

Why had he slept so soundly, he wondered. Had it been the past weeks of hard work, the restless nights in Atlanta, or the full night's sleep he lost while he was a guest of Big Luke, when he was in Macon? Neither, he decided. It was the relief just hearing from Charlene.

Joe Ray dressed and descended the stairs into the lobby. He'd have just enough time for a quick bite of breakfast, then, he must rent a carriage to take him to the school. After he finished eating, he stepped onto the street, only to find a carriage discharging passengers.

"My luck has changed," he determined, when he recognized the driver as being the one whom he had hired earlier in the week. Joe Ray boarded the carriage and asked the driver to take him back to the school where they found Charlene.

"Why so happy this morning?" the driver inquired. "You seem much different than the young man I encountered a few days ago."

Joe Ray told the driver of the happenings of the last few days. He also told him of the devastation the war brought to their plantation and about how much he wanted to build a life with Charlene.

The driver listened with sympathetic ears, and by the time they completed the forty-five minute ride, the driver had learned a great deal about his passenger, including the fact that he had very little money.

As if by fate, Joe Ray reached the school at exactly ten o'clock. He found Charlene sitting on one of the lawn benches in the shade of one of the huge oak trees that decorated the school grounds.

"Could you wait for a little while?" he asked the driver. "I may have further need of your services."

Leaving the driver in the carriage, he slowly approached the bench where Charlene was waiting.

"Please forgive me for my rudeness," she began. "I had no idea that you had not received any of my letters."

It was several seconds before Joe Ray could respond. He was so overcome by her beauty that he was dumbfounded. The last few months only added to her charm. She was much more mature than when she left and came to Atlanta.

"That's alright," he heard himself say. "You had no way of knowing about your letters."

Joe Ray noticed there were several other ladies sitting idly on the lawn.

"I have the driver waiting," he said.to Charlene. "Is it possible we could go for a ride through Atlanta?"

"I was hoping you had something like that in mind,"

she responded. "I have already asked the head mistress for a leave of absence for the day."

"Just a moment," he said to Charlene, and he strolled back to where the driver was waiting.

"Miss Charlene has consented to join me for a ride through Atlanta," he said to the driver. "I only have ten dollars above what I need for my trip back home, so drive us around until we have used up the entire amount. And please don't let the young lady know of my financial situation."

Joe Ray went back to where Charlene was sitting and politely took her by the hand and led her to where the carriage was waiting.

"The lady has consented to show me Atlanta," he said as he helped Charlene into the buggy. "So, lead off in the direction of your choosing," he said, winking at the driver.

"I understand, sir," the driver answered as he looked back and smiled at the young couple.

For the next three hours, they rode the streets of the city. This time with Charlene reminded Joe Ray of the many hours they spent at the oak grove on her father's plantation. She told him that during her first few months in school, she had written to him twice every week, but after receiving no answer, she quit writing.

They agreed that her father must be resposible for his not receiving her letters. By two o'clock in the afternoon, Joe Ray determined that she was not interested in anyone else, and asked if she would still marry him.

"Marry you!" she said with so much excitement that

it caused the driver to look back at them. "Why, I would marry you right now, right this moment, Joe Ray. As a matter of fact, I think that's what we should do.

What do you think, Joe Ray? Why don't we get married right now? All we have to do is acquire a license and find us a preacher. Reverend Warren is the Chaplain at our school and I'm sure he would be happy to perform the ceremony."

Hardly believing what he heard, Joe Ray asked, "Are you serious, Charlene? Would you marry me this afternoon?"

"As serious as General Sherman was when he marched through Georgia," said Charlene. "Before darkness covers Atlanta this day, we'll be Mr. and Mrs. Joe Ray Franklin. To the courthouse on Peachtree Street," she instructed the driver.

The shower of excitement that filled Joe Ray, soon turned to a storm of panic. Suddenly, he remembered he had no money to purchase a license, or to pay the preacher.

"Are you sure you want to get married today?' Joe Ray stammered. "Don't you think ...?"

He was interrupted by the loud noise the driver was making as he pretended to clear his throat. Suddenly, the carriage pulled to the edge of the street and came to a stop.

"Dadburn shoe done come loose again," the driver said, as he picked up the horse's front foot. "Would you mind giving me a hand, sir?" he said to Joe Ray. "These cobblestone streets sure take their toll on the heads of horseshoe nails."

Joe Ray jumped from the carriage and walked to the

77

front of the horse, where the driver was standing with the horse's hoof in his hand. At first glance, he could see that the horseshoe was still securely fastened..

Before he could speak, the driver said, "Some predicament you got yourself in now, young man."

He continued before Joe Ray could speak. "I could not help overhearing your conversation with Miss Charlene. And knowing of your tragedies from our earlier conversations, reminds me some of my own earlier days. You see, I once lived on a beautiful plantation myself, which was also destroyed during the war. Having to leave that place and come to the city was the hardest thing me and my Missus has ever had to do in our whole lives. That's how I ended up here in Atlanta, driving this here buggy for hire. So, you see, it is not hard for me to understand how it is when you're in a bad situation."

"But, how an I ever going to explain to Charlene?" Joe Ray asked in a low voice.

"Seems to me like you ain't got no time for explaining nothing, right now," the old black man stated. "Seems to me like you barely got time to get ready for a wedding."

"But, how in the name of thunder ...?

"You ain't got no time for buts, neither, as I see it," the driver interrupted and slipped five crisp, new ten dollar bills into Joe Ray's hand.

Joe Ray opened his mouth to express his thanks, but no words would come out because he was so overcome by the kindness, he had just been shown.

"'Peers like that shoe was alright after all,' the driver

said as both he and Joe Ray climbed back into the buggy.

Within minutes, the carriage came to a stop in front of the courthouse on Peachtree Street.

"I'll wait," the driver said as both, Joe Ray and Charlene started inside.

Things were happening faster than Joe Ray could comprehend. By six o'clock, all arrangements had been made, and he and Charlene were back at the school, standing in the center of the large entrance foyer.

In front of them, the Reverend Warren was saying, "I now pronounce you man and wife," and added, "you may kiss the bride."

The part about "you may kiss the bride," brought giggles from Charlene's classmates, who were in attendance. So, immediately after receiving congratulations and best wishes from Reverend Warren and her classmates, the newlyweds were back in the carriage and on their way to the hotel on Peachtree Street.

When they arrived at the hotel, Joe Ray said to the driver, "Thank you, sir, for helping us make this a most wonderful day." His meaning needed no explanation. "And please be here in the morning to take me to the station in time to catch the train to Macon."

When Joe Ray entered the lobby with his arm around Charlene, he received a questioning stare from the clerk behind the desk.

"My new bride will be spending the night with me, sir," Joe Ray said as he and Charlene disappeared on their way to their room.

Once in their room, the plans for the future began to unfold. Joe Ray learned that Charlene would be through her schooling in two weeks. They decided it would be best if her father did not know of their marriage until after her return to the plantation.

Joe Ray assured her that the restoration of the mansion would be completed by the time she arrived back in Dublin. He was certain he could have the proceeds from the sale of the cotton by then, and it would be too late for her father to interfere.

The night for the newlyweds passed much too quickly. Before they realized it, it was time for Joe Ray to leave if he was going to catch the train. And too, Charlene had to return to her classes in order to be ready for her graduation.

When they exited the hotel, their driver was waiting as Joe Ray knew he would be. On the way to the station, plans were made for Joe Ray to pick up Charlene in Dublin upon her arrival from Atlanta. They agreed that together, they would go to her father, and only then, would he know of their marriage.

Almost as soon as they arrived at the station, it was time for Joe Ray to board the train. He gave his new bride a final good-bye embrace, and asked the driver if he would please see her back to the school.

"Most assuredly, I will," the driver answered. "I will watch after her as if she were my own."

Joe Ray extended his arm to shake hands with the driver.

"I will always be grateful to you, sir," he said. "I

don't know how I can ever repay your kindness, but someday, surely I can find a way. Is there anything you really need? And, what are you called?"

"Driver Viney," the wrinkled old black man answered. "Just Driver Viney. And, the only thing I need, young man, is to get me and my Missus out of this city. We belong back on a plantation. We are both growing old and neither of us wants to die here in Atlanta. It is our dream that we be buried in the cotton fields where we were born. As for repaying me, just seeing the two of you so happy, is pay enough."

Squeezing the old black hand, which he still held, Joe Ray repeated his former statement. "Someday, I shall find a way."

Chapter Nine
The Storm

"All aboard," he heard the conductor call. "Last train to Macon."

Within minutes, Joe Ray was out of Atlanta, heading south, toward Macon. It was early and he was very tired. He dreaded the day which lay before him. First, he would have to pick up Luther in Macon, and he'd better be at the station, Joe Ray said to himself. Then, there was the long trip on to Dublin, and finally, the buggy to the plantation. It would be a long day and it would be late when they got home. But, he knew the old, run-down slave shacks would be a welcome sight. This was the last thing Joe Ray remembered just before he fell asleep.

He did not know how long he'd been sleeping, but he was awakened by the clang of the metal caused by the slack in the couplings, as the train came to a halt. As he peered out of the window and seeing the Macon depot, he realized he had reached the end of the first leg of his journey.

Now, to find Luther, he thought, and I'll be on my way again. He stepped from the train and onto the platform where other passengers were waiting to board. Luther was nowhere in sight. Joe Ray made several trips around the depot, but Luther could not be found. He approached the ticket agent and gave a description of Luther, as best he could, but was informed by the agent that he had seen no one resembling the person Joe Ray described.

"I'll bet that crazy black boy is still at Big Luke's Place," he said under his breath. "I think I'll go down there and hang him, provided somebody ain't hung him already."

Joe Ray walked the short distance to Luke's Place and went inside. He approached the huge black man who had been their waiter on his previous visit. He was still wearing the same blood-spattered apron he wore when Joe Ray was there earlier.

"Do you remember me?" he inquired of Big Luke, when he was close enough to be heard over the sound of the piano.

"Yeah," answered Luke. "Yo're de one dat come in heah wif dat black feller a few nights ago, de one dat come to win all dat poker money."

"That's right," answered Joe Ray. "Do you know his whereabouts?"

"Shore do," Luke answered. "De law men done picked him up night 'fore last."

"What do you mean, the law men picked him up?" Joe Ray questioned. "What's Luther been into, now?"

"He wuz causin' a big ruckus in heah wif some fellers he said wuz cheatin' an' I had to put a few knuckle bumps on his head an' throw him out in de alley. Las' time I seed him, two law men wuz totin' him off down t'ward the jail."

"And where is the jail?" Joe Ray asked.

"Right straight down de street 'bout ten more buildins," Big Luke informed him. "Guess I ought to know, 'cause most of their business come from heah."

Joe Ray thanked him and made his way in the direction Big Luke described. When he entered the jail, he saw a large-built white gentleman sitting behind a desk. The man was wearing a faded pair of overalls with a badge pinned to one of the suspenders.

"Are you the man in charge?" Joe Ray asked.

"Depends on what I'm supposed to be in charge of," the officer replied.

Joe Ray stated his business and asked whether or now Luther had been locked up.

"Shore has," the officer stated, "and 'less he knows somebody with a lot of money, he's gonna stay locked up for a mighty long time."

"How much money we talking about?" Joe Ray asked.

"Three hundred and fifty dollars," the officer informed him.

"Hell, who did he kill?" Joe Ray wanted to know.

"He didn't kill nobody," the officer stated. "But, he shore as hell done a lot of other stuff. Let's see, there's a

85

twenty-five dollar fine for drunk in public, a ten-dollar fine for disturbing the peace, ten dollars for resisting arrest, and ten dollars for cussing a officer of the law, meaning me.

And there's two hundred and ninety-five dollars to replace all that furniture over at Big Luke's he wuz the cause of gettin' tore up. I shore hope you come to get him out, 'cause he's caused more trouble that half a dozen of these city black fellers do."

Joe Ray explained to the officer that he did not have the money to get Luther released. He did, however, explain that he would have the money within a few days, when he sold his cotton. After a great deal of persuasion, Joe Ray convinced the officer to release Luther to his custody, provided he would sign papers stating that the amount of his release would be paid within two weeks.

After the officer prepared the paper to which Joe Ray applied his signature, the officer went through a door behind his desk and shortly reappeared with Luther.

"How'd yo' manage to git me outta heah?" Luther wanted to know.

"By promising to pay ten times more than you're worth," Joe Ray answered. "I signed my name to this paper here, promising to pay your bill as soon as I sell my cotton."

Pointing to the document on top of the desk, Joe Ray added, "This paper says I'm going to pay in cash and you're going to pay me back in blood if you have to, but you're going to pay me back."

Luther stared at the paper to which Joe Ray referred and promised to repay it in full.

"I ain't never gonna play no more poker in my whole life and I ain't never gonna steal nuttin' else neither. Yo' got my word on dat, Joe Ray. Now, where's my whittlin' knife?" he asked the officer.

"What whittlin' knife you talkin' 'bout, boy?" the officer asked.

"The whittlin' knife that other lawman took offen me the night yo' all locked me up." Luther said.

"I don't know, but I guess its around here some-where," the officer stated, as he started looking through the drawers of his desk.

Luther sat down on the front of the desk and waited for the officer to continue his search for the knife. Then, suddenly he jumped up from where he was sitting.

"Come on, les' git outta heah, Joe Ray," he stated, heading for the door. "Dat ol' knife wouldn't be worth much anyway, an' 'sides, ain't it 'bout time fer us to git on dat train?"

Joe Ray realized Luther was right and started to fol-low him into the street. The officer followed them to the door and yelled as they were leaving.

"You make shore you get me that money back heah in two weeks, you heah? I wouldn' let you fellers off so easy anyhow, if you hadn't told me your place was next to John McClanahan's. That way, I'll know where to come and get you if you don't pay."

Joe Ray started on up the street with Luther close behind.

"Step it up," Joe Ray said to him. "We have to hurry

or we'll be late. You better not make me miss that train.
You've already caused me enough trouble for one day."

Joe Ray and Luther reached the station with very little
time to spare. Upon reaching the depot, they raced to the
ticket window and Joe Ray said to the agent, "Two tickets
to Dublin, please."

The agent reached him the tickets as he stated, "That
will be four dollars, sir." Joe Ray handed the man two one-
dollar bills and waited for Luther to produce the money for
his fare.

"Hurry up, Luther," he said. "The train is about ready
to pull out and they ain't gonna wait on us all day. Don't tell
me you ain't got two dollars left?"

"I ain't got nuttin' left," Luther stated. "Dat's what
de fight over at Big Luke's wuz all 'bout. Dem two fellers
frum Boston cheated me out of ever penny I had. I wish't I
could git me some more money, so I could stay heah in
Macon frum now on," he added.

"I guess they cheated you out of the money you took
from Ma Mattie too, didn't they?"

"Shore did," Luther exclaimed. "Dat's what made
me so mad."

"Damn you, Luther," Joe Ray growled, reaching the
ticket agent another two dollars.

"I ought to leave you right hear in Macon, but I know
if I did, they'd lock you back up and I'd have to sell the
whole plantation to pay off what you'd owe next time."

He grabbed Luther by the shirt sleeve and held onto
him until they boarded the train which was already moving

slowly away from the station.

"See what you done now, Luther?" he said as he looked around at the half-dozen other Negro passengers. "You done caused me to have to ride back here with you black folks instead of up where I belong."

Joe Ray seated himself on the boxcar floor just as one of the Negro men across from him pulled a deck of cards from his pocket.

"Hey, yo' got any money left?" Luther asked Joe Ray. "If yo' have, me an' yo'll git in dis poker game and I'll win dat two dollars back dat I owes yo' fer my ticket."

"What you mean, that two dollars you owe me for the ticket? What about the three hundred and fifty dollars you owe me for getting you out of jail?"

"Yo' ain't got no need of worrin' 'bout dat three hunnert an' fifty dollars," Luther replied. "I done seen to takin' care of dat," he said, as he pulled the piece of paper that Joe Ray signed from his pocket.

Joe Ray took the paper from Luther and pointed to a place beside him on the floor.

"Sit yourself down right there, Luther," he said, "and if you even mention playing poker again, I'm gonna throw you right off this train. And I'm gonna do it when we're at top speed, too."

Luther seated himself beside Joe Ray and watched as the other men began to play.

"How much money yo' plannin' on gittin' for dat cotton, anyway?" he asked.

"I don't know exactly," was Joe Ray's answer.

"There'll be enough to pay off the loan at the bank and to send the money back to Macon to pay your fine, and maybe a good bit left over. But, you ain't gonna get none to get in no poker game, Luther, so you might as well get that out of your head."

"How yo' go 'bout sellin' dat cotton an' gittin' de money, anyhow?" Luther wanted to know.

Joe Ray explained to Luther that each plantation owner brought their cotton to different shipping points from Macon to Savannah. He explained that many more rail cars were needed to take the cotton to the seaports.

"The buyers bid for the cotton once it reaches Savannah," he continued. "The cotton auction is always on Wednesday and we receive our money when the train makes its run from Savannah on Friday."

"Yo' mean dey haul de cotton to Savannah all week long an' den dey haul a load of money back on Frid'y?" Luther asked.

"That's about it," Joe Ray answered.

"Yo' mean in cash money?" Luther asked.

"Sure, in cash," Joe Ray replied. "What did you think they would pay us with, Luther? Horseshoes?"

Luther surveyed the small piles of money in front of each of the men who were gambling just a few feet away from where he and Joe Ray were seated.

"A feller shore could play a lot of poker wif all dat money dat's comin' back in dat train, couldn't he, Joe Ray?" Luther said.

"Yeah," was Joe Ray's reply. "I guess there'd be

enough to last you the most part of a week, Luther."

"Yo' shore dat money always comes back on Frid'y?" Luther continued to question, as he scooted himself closer to where the men were gambling.

"I'm sure," Joe Ray said, as he stretched himself along the boxcar floor and lay his head on his travel bag.

For the next few hours, Joe Ray listened to the whine of the wheels and pondered the happenings of the last few days, while Luther contented himself watching the poker game.

Shortly after sundown, Joe Ray and Luther were back at the station in Dublin, where they found Old Ben waiting.

"Better hurry," Ole Ben warned, "from the looks of dem skies, dey's gonna be a bad storm on us afore we git home."

"I believe you're right," Joe Ray said as he and Luther jumped on the back of the buggy.

"How wuz yo' trip?" Old Ben asked as he turned the horse and headed in the direction of the plantation.

"It was great, but I'll tell you all about it later," said Joe Ray, being interrupted by a large bolt of lightning.

"An' what 'bout yo', Luther? he asked.

"Oh, nuttin' outta de ordinary," was Luther's response. His answer was followed by a deep roll of thunder that seemed to be directly over their heads.

"Somebody up there is trying to tell him something about all that lying," Joe Ray thought as he scooted himself up tight against the seat to get what shelter he could from the down-pouring rain that began to fall.

Ole Ben whipped up the horses to increase their pace, but the trip home was through one of the worst storms Joe Ray had ever encountered. The constant roll of thunder and continuous whip-like lightning flashes made this a fearful time. By the time they reached home, the road had become deeply rutted and the water that covered the cotton fields was more than ankle deep.

As the buggy approached the front of Joe Ray's shack, he jumped off without Ole Ben having to stop. As he opened the door to his dwelling, he could see the carriage carrying Ole Ben and Luther disappear into the delapidated old barn. The storm continued far into the night and Joe Ray was glad to be home. He removed his rain-soaked clothing and piled them in a heap at the foot of his bed, and slipped beneath the covers of his cot.

"Did you have a good time?" he heard his father say from his own bed on the other side of the room.

"Sure did," Joe Ray answered. "I'll tell you all about it in the morning. Tonight, I'm too tired."

Soon, he fell asleep.

The next morning, Joe Ray was awakened abruptly by a loud pounding on their door.

"Get up, get up! Somethin' terrible has happened!" Joe Ray was hearing. He knew it was Sara's voice. He slipped into his cold, wet trousers from the night before and stepped our onto the porch. Before he could say a word, Sara began to speak.

"Dat was a terrible bad storm last night," she said, "an' one of dem streaks of lightnin' done killed Mr. John."

92

"You mean John McClanahan?" Joe Ray asked.

"Dat's right," Sara went on. "One of de black folks from de 'Clanahan plantation jus' come by an' tole me and I knowed yo' an' Boss Bill would want to know."

"How did it happen?" Joe Ray asked.

"Seems Mr. John wuz out tryin' out a new horse he'd jus' bought," Sara said, getting more excited as she talked. "He got hisself caught in dat bad storm. One of dem flashes of lightnin' caused de horse to bolt an' throwed Mr. John off, right on his head.

Dey say his neck wuz broke slap dab in two. Dey didn't even find him 'til after daylight dis mornin' an' dey said his body wuz most covered up wif mud. De buryin' gonna be ten o'clock in de mornin', so dey say. I knowed yo' and Boss Bill would won' to know. Miss Charlene shore gonna be saddened not to be heah to see her daddy put away."

Joe Ray's feelings were mixed. Although he was sad for Charlene's loss, he could not help but feel relief to know that John McClanahan could no longer do anything to keep them apart. He longed to go to Atlanta to be with Charlene, but he knew that was impossible. There was just too much work to be done.

Although this was Sunday, and it was not customary for any work to be done on the Lord's Day, he knew he would have to make an exception. In order for all the cotton to be at the railhead in Dublin, for shipment Tuesday morning, they would have to begin loading the wagons at once. If he did not meet his appointed shipping day, he might not be able to get another for two weeks, and that would be too late.

93

His bank note was due the following Monday, and it must be paid. There would be no exceptions, the banker had taken great pains to explain. If only the rain would let up, the task would be much easier, but from the looks of the dense cloud covering still rolling in from the north, the possibility did not seem likely. Everyone on the plantation knew the dilemma facing them and they all worked with every bit of energy they could muster.

It was not until noon that day that the first canvas-covered wagons were on their way. It was three miles through the cotton fields to the railroad tracks, along the river, and then, another half-mile further, following the tracks to the station. The first trip would be the easiest, for as the wagons traveled back and forth, the ruts in the sandy clay would become deeper and deeper, thus making each trip more difficult than the one before.

"If only we had more horses," Joe Ray complained, but soon put the thought out of his mind. Once, there had been many horses on the plantation, but each time one became too old for use, he was sold or just died and was never replaced. The five teams they now used were all that were left.

By nightfall, only two trips were completed, and many more would be required.

"I really think we're defeated," Joe Ray said to his father as he drove the mud-splattered wagon up along the side of the huge cotton storage shed. "With only one day left, and with this down-pouring rain, there just ain't no way."

"What do you mean, just one more day?" Boss Bill

questioned. "We got two whole nights, ain't we? Have Mattie and the other women whip up something to eat while we load these wagons again, and have everybody gather up all the lanterns there are on the place. We ain't whipped yet."

"There ain't no way, Boss Bill," Joe Ray continued. "Even if we work night and day, we ain't going to be able to get all the cotton to Dublin by Tuesday. We just ain't got enough horses."

Overhearing their conversation, Luther asked, "Iffen yo' had some more horses to pull some of our other wagons, yo' could do it, couldn't yo', Joe Ray?"

"Yeah, and if a bullfrog had wings, he could sleep with the crows instead of the catfish, Luther," was Joe Ray's reply.

"Humph," grunted Luther. "I shore would like to see a crow sleepin' wif a catfish."

By the time the five wagons were reloaded, it was far into the night. Boss Bill and Joe Ray were sitting in the storage shed with the Negroes, eating the food Mattie, Sara, and the others had prepared while the wagons were being loaded.

"Where's Luther," someone asked, realizing he was the only one missing.

"He probably snuk off womewhere and went to sleep," commented Ole Ben. "Yo' know how Luther is. He ain't never been much fer workin' in de daylight, let 'lone doin' anythin' after night."

When everyone finished eating, Joe Ray walked to

the entrance to the shed to survey the clouds, hoping there would be some sign of the end of the drenching rain. As he stepped from the shed, he could see a lantern approaching from the direction of the McClanahan place.

"Who in the world could that be, out in the middle of the night like this?" he asked of no one in particular.

"Sounds like a whole crowd, iffen yo're askin' me." Ole Ben replied, hearing what soulded like the rattle of chains coming nearer.

Joe Ray waited for the light until it was barely a few feet away, before realizing what he had been watching.

"Heah's dem horses yo' said yo' needed, Joe Ray. Ever one of dem already got de harness on an' ready fer workin'"

Joe Ray raised the lantern far enough above his head so as not to be blinded by the light. Sure enough, there sat Luther on his mule, holding a rope in one hand. The rope was attached to a whole string of horses. Ten, to be exact.

"De way I seen it, we got five more good wagons, so all we needed wuz ten more horses," Luther grinned.

"You done stole ten of John McClanahan's best work horses." Joe Ray scolded.

"Didn't I git 'nough?" Luther asked, still grinning. "I wuz shore ten wuz all we needed. 'Sides, ol' man 'Clanahan ain't gonna be needin' 'em anyhow. He's layin' over there in dat pine box, stiff as a poker. Dey's shore a lot of folks over there, too, but dey's all inside de house 'cause of all dis rain. I could of stole de back porch iffen I'd had a mind to."

"What are we ever going to do with him, Boss Bill?" Joe Ray asked, turning to his father.

"We're going to let him help us load up five more wagons," was Boss Bill's answer, "just as soon as we can get them horses hitched up."

"I'm shore glad he wasn't twins," Mattie said to Boss Bill in an apologetic tone, as Joe Ray and the others began hooking the newly acquired teams to five more wagons.

"Me, too, Mattie," Boss Bill laughed, giving her a gentle pat on the shoulder. "There ain't no way in the world we could have used twenty horses."

Everyone worked throughout the night, and until late evening the following day in the never ceasing rain.

Just as the last rays of sunlight were giving way to darkness, the last of the cotton from the Franklin plantation was being unloaded onto the platform at the station, ready for shipping the following morning, when the rain suddenly stopped.

"Well, I'll be damned," said Luther. "I wuz hopin' dem horses would be able to swim home, but now, I figger dey'll jus' have to walk."

Although totally exhausted, everyone found energy to laugh at what Luther said.

When everyone found a place in the wagons, the caravan began the slow return through the mud-covered cotton fields to the Franklin plantation.

Chapter Ten
Luther Quits Stealing

The next three days were spent in total relaxation. Even the work on the mansion was postponed. It was still ten days until Charlene's return and Joe Ray knew there was plenty of time to do what was needed for its completion.

On Friday, Luther was up early. When Joe Ray awoke and emerged from his shack, he found him sitting on the edge of the porch, holding a rope attached to his mule.

"I guess I know what you're going to do, Luther," Joe Ray stated. "You're going fishing."

"I goin' fishin' 'til dark," Luther answered. "Den, I goin" frog huntin'. Dat is, iffen yo' an' Boss Bill will give me de loan of yo' musketball pistol."

At first, Joe Ray started to object, but remembering all Luther had done to help, he did not know how he could refuse.

99

"Does it really shoot?" Luther inquired as Joe Ray came from inside once more and reached him the pistol.

"Sure it does, Luther. But, I bet you ain't never shot a pistol before in your life."

"I'll figger hit out. Sides, dem frogs I been seein' is so big, I don't figger I can miss."

"Yo' shore dis is de day de train gonna brang all dat money up from Savannah?" Luther asked as he put the pistol in the front pocket of his overalls and got onto his mule.

"Yessir, it sure is," Joe Ray answered. "It sure is."

"Den, yo' be rich 'fore dark, Joe Ray," Luther said, grinning and started riding off toward the river.

"Strange," Joe Ray thought, and Luther rode away. "Reckon why he had his mule harnessed and reckon what he was doing with that rope tied to one of the hames?"

Well, it don't matter," he said to himself as he went back inside to prepare for the trip the Dublin. "I could stand here all day trying to figure out Luther."

Shortly after noon, Joe Ray left for Dublin to pick up the cash from their cotton. Boss Bill insisted that he go alone. He knew his father did this only to let him know that he had confidence in his ability to handle such responsibility.

Knowing that he would arrive at the Dublin station before the train was due, Joe Ray decided to stop at the bend of the river to kill some time, talking to Luther. When he reached their favorite fishing hole, however, Luther was no where to be seen. Not knowing which direction he might have gone, Joe Ray made no effort to search for him.

Instead, he seated himself on one of the rails and began watching the water below. The rain, the last three days, had caused the water to be troubled. The river was higher and moving more rapidly than he had ever known it to be in years.

Joe Ray waited until almost time for the train to arrive, before he remounted his saddle horse to ride the remaining half-mile to the station. He arrived only moments before the train.

When the train arrived, two men carrying shotguns, stepped onto the platform. Joe Ray was soon to learn that these men were railroad guards used for security when large amounts of cash were shipped on the train. Each of the guards stood on the platform, while a third man entered the station, carrying a large leather case.

"Here are the proceeds for the cotton shipped from this station," Joe Ray heard the man carrying the case, say to the agent.

"I bet you're carrying a fortune on this trip." the agent inquired of the guard.

"One of the largest, ever," was the guard's reply.

The agent counted the money while more wood and water were being taken onto the train. When enough of both were aboard, the two guards followed the third man onto the train, and within a minute, it pulled away from the station.

"Wonder how many more places, between here and Macon, money will be unloaded?" Joe Ray thought as he entered the station to pick up the cash that was due him.

"Looks as if you did alright," the agent said to him, looking over some papers he held in his hand. "Over seven thousand dollars, it says here."

"Over seven thousand dollars!" Joe Ray began to figure. "Why, that was enough to repay their loan at the bank, pay for Luther's hell-raising in Macon, (which he intended to do, although Luther had stolen the note,) feed everyone on the plantation for the next year, and buy seed for their next crop. One could not ask for more," he decided as he left the station and headed back to share the news with Boss Bill and the others.

He followed the tracks alongside the river to where the road turned towards their plantation. Just as he approached the river bend, he heard a shotgun blast.

"That can't be Luther," he thought. Then, remembering the shotguns the guards were carrying, he decided to investigate.

He had gone little more than a hundred yards until he could see the rear of the train. Realizing something was wrong, Joe Ray speeded up his pace.

Just as he rode up to where the train was stopped, he saw Luther's mule, still tied to a log, which lay on the tracks. Luther was grasping a low hanging sycamore limb with his body half-submerged in the rapidly flowing river. Blood ws dripping from his back into the water below. In his other hand, he was clutching a leather bag. Joe Ray recognized it as the one the guard carried into the station just minutes earlier.

"Drop it!" he heard one of the guards yell, as he fired

a second time.

Joe Ray saw Luther release his hold on the limb and disappear from view into the muddy water of the Oconee River.

"Good Lord!" he gulped. "Luther's robbed the train."

For the next two days, everyone for miles around, helped the railway employees search the banks of the river, but Luther was not to be found. Nor, was the bag that had gone into the water with him. They learned after the search was abandoned, that the bag contained over one hundred thousand dollars.

Work on the mansion was completed the following week, but there was no celebration. Boss Bill and Joe Ray repaid the bank loan, but that, too, did little to erase the hurt of their loss.

Truly, Luther would be missed. There was no burying, nor was any funeral ever held, for Luther's body was never found.

"The Lord does work in mysterious ways," Boss Bill said the day the railroad gave up its search. "I guess He knew that if there was a funeral, the preacher would have to tell a lie, 'cause Luther never did anything that was honest."

Joe Ray was restless for the next few days, for there was little to do. The day before Charlene was to arrive, he was sitting on the porch, anticipating what life would be like with his new bride and remembering all the carefree days he and Luther had shared.

Then, as if she knew what Joe Ray was thinking, Luther's old mule appeared.

"Bet you would like to go fishin', wouldn't you, girl? That's what you'd be doing if Luther was here." He spoke more to himself than to the mule.

Then, realizing he had nothing better to occupy his time, decided that was just what he would do. He quickly retrieved his pole from inside the shack, and before he had time for a second thought, he was on his way. He did not even bother to bridle Luther's mule, for he knew that she knew where to go.

Just as he expected, the mule headed straight for the bend of the river. Joe Ray found fishing worms beneath the moist grass sod that was left when the water receded. Baiting his hook, he threw the line into the muddy water. He seated himself beneath one of the large trees and waited for something to bite. Two hours passed and darkness was drawing near, but nothing had caused movement on his line.

"Time to go home, girl," he said to Sadie Mae, who was chomping the tall grass beside the tracks, where Luther normally tied her. Joe Ray picked up his pole , but was unable to pull in his line. He gave a hard tug in order to pull the hook free. Then, he realized he was dragging something in the water.

"Must be a turtle," he thought. "I guess that's the reason no fish would bite."

He pulled his line tight and began to back up the bank in order to pull the turtle out of the water. Suddenly, the object which was attached to his hook began to rise up to the surface.

What Joe Ray saw next caused his heart to start

pounding, for on the end of his line was the case he saw disappear with Luther into the river. He pulled the case to the water's edges and inspected the contents. There before him was more money than he ever dreamed existed.

"Over a hundred thousand dollars," he remembered hearing one of the guards say. But, the money did not belong to him. He must give it back.

"Why should I give it back? he questioned himself.

Had they, too, not suffered many losses in the past, and no one ever offered to give them anything back. Was this not the money that belonged to the Yankee upper-crust, and were they not responsible for the loss of their plantation? And what if the railroad must take the loss? Could they not afford it?

"And besides, who deserved it more than those of us at the plantation? And what a way to begin a life with Charlene," he said to himself.

His mind was spinning so fast that he did not know what to do. Hide it for now, he decided, and do something later.

Joe Ray waited until it was dark enough that he was sure he could not be seen before he left the banks of the river. When he determined it was safe, he got onto the back of Luther's mule and headed toward the plantation.

As if from habit, Sadie Mae did not stop until she was inside the fallen-down old barn, where she had always been kept.

Feeling relieved that he had not been seen, Joe Ray began to look around for a safe hiding place. Seeing an old wooden grain box at one end of the barn, he decided it would be safe enough until he had time to find a more secure place.

He removed some pieces of harness from the top of the box and raised the lid. He placed the case inside, but was unable to close the box. Not enough space in here, he thought, so he felt inside to determine what could be removed to make the room he needed. It was too dark to see, but he could feel a bundle on top of whatever else the box contained. Removing the bundle was enough to enable the lid to close. Satisfied that the money was hidden well enough, he picked up the bundle and proceeded to his shack.

Once inside, Joe Ray was able to make out what it was that he took from the grain box. There on top of the bundle was a letter addressed to him. To Joe Ray Franklin, Dublin, Georgia, it read. The return address was: Miss Charlene McClanahan, c/o Atlanta Academy, Number 11 Maple Street, Atlanta, Georgia.

"I wish he was alive, so I could kill him myself, and I would, too! I'd kill him graveyard dead for this," Joe Ray was saying as he paced the floor.

"What's got you so upset?" Boss Bill wanted to know. "If you don't calm down, you could die from anger."

"I'd kill him for this," he said as he told his father what he found. "No wonder he wanted to go fishing every Friday. He was going on to Dublin to get my mail. I knew he wanted me to go fishing with him all the time, and he was always telling me to forget about Charlene and go with him to Macon. But, I never thought he would do anything as dishonest as this."

106

"Where did he have them hid all this time?" Boss Bill asked.

"He hid them in that old, old, uh, he hid them out in the cotton shed." Joe Ray lied, not wanting to mention the grain box, even to his father.

"Too late to do anything about it now, unless you want to give that railroad guard a reward for killing him." Boss Bill added.

Joe Ray examined the letters, finding the seals still unbroken. He opened the one with the earliest postmark and began to read. He read every letter at least twice in the order they were written. By the time he finished the final letter, which was postmarked only one month earlier, his anger toward Luther only increased. All those months of worry had been for naught.

No wonder she treated him so unkindly when he first arrived at the Atlanta Academy. Assuming that he received her letters and simply refused to answer, she must have thought it brazen for him to appear as if he had taken her for granted.

"So be it. All's well that ends well, I suppose. And tomorrow, Charlene will be home and I can explain everything more clearly then," he told himself.

Joe Ray placed the letters on the floor beneath the head of his bed and put out the oil lamp on the table near the center of the room. He slipped into his bed, tired from all the stress brought on by the surprises of the day. Over a hundred thousand dollars, he thought, just before he surrendered his body to mental fatigue.

Chapter Eleven
Charlene Comes Home

"Swing low, swing low, Sweet Chariot, comin' fo' to carry me home," Mattie's voice kept getting louder and louder, until it reached a pitch high enough to arouse Joe Ray from his sleep. When he was fully awake, he slipped into his cotton working overalls, which was the nearest piece of clothing on hand, and went outside to see what was making Mattie so happy.

"Mornin' Joe Ray," she said as he appeared in the doorway, pulling his suspenders up over his shoulders.

"Seein' as how dis is the day Miss Charlene is coming home, I knowed yo' would want to git yoursef outta dat bed early. Boss Bill said he done got yo're eatin's on de table, an' Old Ben tol' me he would hook de horse to the buggy quick as yo' give him de go 'head.

Heah's yo' bes' shirt to go wif dat new outfit yo' bought when yo' wuz up in 'Lanta. I done ironed ever

109

wrinkle out of it so yo' could have it fresh dis mornin'. See, its slick as a newborn baby's behind," she said, reaching the shirt to Joe Ray.

"Thank you, Mattie," Joe Ray told her as she turned and started to walk away.

"If they ain't a weddin' 'round heah 'fore de moon change again, I shore am agoin' to be s'prised," he heard her chuckle, speaking more to herself than anyone else.

Not knowing of their marriage while he was in Atlanta, Joe Ray let her amuse herself in anticipation of the coming event.

He found it hard not to share his secret with Mattie, for she had been the nearest thing to a mother he had ever known. But, he and Charlene agreed that only Boss Bill should know until they could break the news to her family, especially to her father. Now, that John McClanahan was gone, it probably would not matter, but to tell anyone else, he felt would be betrayal.

Anyway, Mattie needed something to take her mind of Luther's death, so if concentrating on his future could help to erase some of her grief, so be it, Joe Ray decided.

Before going back inside, he paused for a moment to admire the newly retored mansion. A work of art, he had to admit, for what was just a few weeks ago, the charred remains of a past era, best forgotten, was now a masterpiece.

The magnificent columns sparkled as the morning sun touched the remaining dew drops that clung to the newly painted surface. The leaves on the gigantic oak trees surrounding the dwelling, were turning many shades of gold and brown, each holding to the mother limb as tightly as nature would allow, for fear that if it let go, it would be swept away by the wind and cease to be part of the view.

"Time to eat, Joe Ray," he heard his father say from inside. "You wouldn't want that train to get to Dublin before you."

Realizing that Boss Bill was right, he went inside and took his usual place at the table.

"What is to become of us, now?" he asked as he started gulping down his food.

"What do you mean? his father asked, looking surprised.

"In a few days, you, Charlene and I will be moving into the mansion," he continued, without slowing his food consumption, "just as soon as we buy the furniture to replace what was destroyed. But, what of Ole Ben and Mattie, and the others. They have worked as hard as you and me, and it seems unfair that only we should reap the rewards."

Boss Bill looked at his son for a long moment without speaking. He was so filled with pride in the young man who sat across from him, it was some time before he could respond. He was grateful his son possessed the characteristic which made him consider the welfare of others.

"The responsibility is yours," he finally heard himself say. "I'm sure you'll do what's right."

Joe Ray finished his breakfast without further conversation. His mind was on how he could reward the others. Reward. He had almost forgotten the money he so

111

painstakingly hid the night before. Maybe some of the money could be used to repay the loyalty the others had extended to him and Boss Bill. One more reason to keep it, he decided.

In a short while, Joe Ray was dressed in the suit he purchased and the clean shirt Mattie so carefully washed and ironed for him. He came out onto the porch to find Ole Ben waiting.

"How could I do without them?" he wondered, thinking of the Negro couple to whom he owed so much. Climbing aboard, Joe Ray realized that Ole Ben had on his best suit.

"Just like yo' said it would be, Joe Ray," his companion was saying. "Yo' said that someday, I would be drivin' yo' 'round like I used to do Boss Bill an' yo' Ma."

Remembering their conversation from months before, he said to Old Ben, "From now on, your only task will be to care for and drive the horses. Your work in the cotton fields has ended."

"Yo' mean that, Joe Ray?" Ole Ben questioned. "Yo' mean I don't has to work in no more cotton?"

"That's right, sir," Joe Ray answered. "From now on, life for you and Mattie will be much easier."

"Thank yo', Joe Ray," he smiled and sat up in the seat as if he were in full command. "I has always prayed for de day when I wouldn't have to work no more cotton."

"Swing low, Sweet Chariot," Ole Ben's deep voice began to chant, "comin' fo' to carry me home."

Joe Ray listened without interrupting, until they

reached the station. The train from Macon pulled into the Dublin station right on schedule.

Charlene stepped onto the platform and threw herself into Joe Ray's waiting arms. "Ain't it awful about Daddy," she began. "I hope you can forgive him for intercepting my letters," she began to sob.

"We'll talk about it later," Joe Ray interrupted. "First, we must let your family know we're married."

Still trying to control her emotions, she nodded her approval, as Joe Ray ushered her to the buggy.

When they arrived at the McClanahan plantation, Charlene went directly inside to find her mother. She was followed by all four of her brothers.

"I'm sorry I was away when Daddy died," Charlene said, embracing her mother, who was sitting in front of a large fireplace, slowly moving back and forth in a rocking chair. Mrs. McClanahan's expression did not change.

"You know I would have come home for the funeral if I could have," Charlene continued, but again, her mother did not acknowledge she even heard her.

"She's been like this ever since Daddy was killed," one of her brothers told her.

Charlene knelt before her chair and placed her hands on the lap of her mother. "Please hear what I'm going to say," Charlene told her. "Joe Ray and I are married."

Still her mother did not respond.

"Well, I'll be damned." It was the voice of her older brother, Bobby as he stomped down the hallway toward the main entrance of the house.

113

"Where are you going?" Charlene asked, running after him.

"I'm going up yonder where Daddy is buried and put my ear to the ground. I know I will be able to hear him turning over in his grave."

"He'll get over it," said Charlene's younger brother, Billy. He assured her with a gentle hug.

"I don't care if he never gets over it," Charlene told him, taking her husband by the hand. "Joe Ray and I are married and there's nothing anyone can do about it now."

Still holding Joe Ray's hand, she led him out of the room.

"We're going to the Franklin plantation," she said. "Tell Mother I'll return later today."

When they were once again in the buggy, Joe Ray turned to Bobby, who stood pouting near the yard gate.

"By the way, thanks for the use of your horses the other day, Bob," he said, pouring salt into the freshly opened wound.

"You mean you were the low-down rascal that stole those horses, and then sent them home still in harness?" Bob said, moving a step or two closer to the buggy.

"No, sir! Dat was Luther," Ole Ben interjected. "But, I 'spose yo're Daddy done had a talk wif him 'bout dat by now. Get up!" he said to the horse, and they were on their way.

As their buggy approached the old slave quarters on the Franklin plantation, everyone began to gather in a small crowd to welcome Joe Ray and Charlene.

When Ole Ben came to a stop in front of the shack where Joe Ray lived with his father, the young man stood up in the buggy and made a gesture to Mattie, indicating he wanted her to come closer. When she did so, he leaned over and whispered something in her ear, so the others could not hear.

"Yo' done what? Yo" tellin' dis ole black soul de truth?" Mattie questioned when Joe Ray had finished.

"Well, ain't life jus' full of s'prises?" she said loud enough for all the others to hear. "De's two young' uns done went off and got theirsefs hitched."

Mattie's announcement brought a roar of approval from everyone on the plantation, especially from Sara.

"I knowed everthin' wuz goin' to be alright," she said, climbing onto the side of the buggy to give Charlene a big squeeze. "Even when Mr. John found out 'bout me sneaking yo' off to meet Mr. Joe Ray an' run us off'n his place, I knowed everthin' gonna be alright."

As the excitement began to die down, Joe Ray and Charlene made their way up the rise toward the mansion. After taking a tour of their new home, the couple relaxed beneath the oak trees on the front lawn.

Since this was the first opportunity the two had to be alone, Joe Ray told her of the events that had taken place. He told her that it was Luther, and not her father, who had stolen the letters. He also informed her of how Luther had been killed, while robbing the train, and of his trouble in Macon.

As late afternoon approached, the couple caught up

on most of the happenings while Charlene was away, and began making decisions on how they should start their life together.

It would be best, they decided, if Charlene stayed with her mother for a few days, until she and Joe Ray could purchase the much needed furniture.

Long before Joe Ray wanted, it was time to take Charlene back to the McClanahan plantation. It had been hard enough not seeing her since they parted in Atlanta, but to be apart and having her such a short distance away, was going to be even worse.

As they drove to the McClanahan plantation, Charlene turned to Joe Ray and began to speak. "Let's go by the grove where we used to meet," she said, blushing.

Without answering, Joe Ray turned the buggy toward their secret place. Once there, he unhooked the horse and tied it to graze. As darkness settled upon the barren cotton fields, the newlyweds disappeared inside one of the storage houses that was practically filled with hay.

"Let's go to Macon tomorrow," Charlene was saying.

Opening his eyes, Joe Ray realized it was far past sunrise the next day. Pulling Charlene back onto the hay beside him, he asked her to repeat what she had said.

"Let's go to Macon tomorrow," she repeated herself, "and buy what we need so we can move into the plantation house right away."

"And on to Atlanta, maybe?" Joe Ray asked. "There's something in Atlanta I want to do."

"Why not?" Charlene giggled, as she ran out into the sunlight and grabbed the rope Joe Ray used to secure the horse the evening before.

Reaching the rope to him, she said, "Now, take me to check on Mama," still giggling, she added, "the very idea, you keeping a southern lady out all night."

Charlene and Joe Ray were to spend their last night apart, for he had plans for moving into the plantation house immediately upon their return from Atlanta.

On his way back home, he decided he was surely going to keep the railroad's money. And, he knew just what he would buy first, for he had not yet bought a ring for Charlene. "I'll have to tell Boss Bill," he determined, "but no one else will ever know."

When he reached home, his father was relaxing in his usual place on the porch in his favorite chair, which was leaning back against the shack. He was looking up the rise, as Joe Ray had seen him do many evenings before. This evening was different, for Boss Bill possessed a look of contentment.

Happy that he found his daddy all alone, Joe Ray began to tell him about the money he found and how he decided he was going to keep it. Not giving Boss Bill time to offer any objections, he continued.

"Think of how much easier life could be, not only for you, Charlene and me, but for everyone on the plantation. We could buy us some fine horses, 'cause Luther ain't going to be around to borrow horses for us no more. And what about Ole Ben and Mattie? They are growing old and

117

I already told Ole Ben he wouldn't have to do no more work in the cotton. And those old, run-down slave shacks, Boss Bill, the black folks have been good to us and they deserve some real nice living quarters."

Boss Bill sat for some time as if he were staring into the future, or maybe he was remembering how their life had been in the past.

Joe Ray said no more, but sat waiting for some sign of approval.

Boss Bill got out of his chair and stepped into the yard. He began surveying the surroundings as if he had never seen them before.

At last, he looked back to where Joe Ray was sitting. A smile began to appear on his weather-beaten face.

"Where you think we ought to build them new quarters?" he asked.

"I'll leave that up to you," he said, embracing his father. "You can figure it out tomorrow. Charlene and I are going to Atlanta."

Joe Ray informed Boss Bill where the money was hidden.

"I have taken some of the bills for our trip," he stated. "But, the rest is soaking wet. Will you see to drying it out?" he asked.

"Yes, sir!" Boss Bill responded.

Chapter Twelve
Joe Ray Repays A Debt

When Joe Ray arrived at the McClanahan plantation the next day, Charlene was ready to go.

"I have all my belongings packed," she said as she threw her arms around him, allowing herself to be lifted into the buggy. "I have brought only what I'll need for our trip," she continued, drawing attention to the two large travel bags her younger brother, Billy, placed in the back of the buggy. "We'll come and get everything else when we return from Atlanta."

"We're only going to be gone for a few days," Joe Ray teased, making fun of the quantity of her baggage, "you sure you brought enough?"

"Mind your manners, Joe Ray Franklin," she said, indicating she was ready to get started.

Ole Ben spoke gently to the horse and the carriage began moving.

"Make sure you're back Monday," Billy called after them. "Remember that's the day Lawyer McCord's gonna read Daddy's will."

"We'll be there," Charlene assured him, as she scooted closer to Joe Ray.

The next two days in Macon were spent shopping for the furniture they needed for the mansion. Each piece, Charlene selected, met with Joe Ray's approval. He knew nothing about things of this nature, so he was grateful for her expertise. As each purchase was made, the merchant was instructed to ship the merchandise on the next train. Joe Ray had made prior arrangements for Boss Bill to receive the furniture at the Dublin station and have it in the mansion when they returned, as a surprise for Charlene.

When the furniture buying was completed, there remained only one business matter to take care of before the trip on to Atlanta. That being, the matter of paying Luther's fine at the Macon jail. Joe Ray left Charlene to do some shopping by herself, desiring to take care of this matter alone.

He entered the building which housed the jail, finding things pretty much as they were nearly two weeks earlier. The officer was relaxed behind his desk, displaying his badge on one of his suspender straps, wearing what Joe Ray believed to be the same pair of overalls he wore in his earlier visit.

"I'm Joe Ray Franklin," he announced, approaching the desk where the officer was sitting. "I'm here to pay the money I owe you."

"I know well who you are," the lawman replied, spitting ambure in the direction of a spittoon, which was sitting beside a potbellied stove.

Surveying the floor around the container, Joe Ray surmised that this was not the only time he had missed.

"I didn't expect on ever seeing you again," the officer continued, "seeing as how that black boy done stole that paper you signed. I know he's the one that stole it, too."

"That's right," Joe Ray answered.

"Wuz he the one that got killed robbing that train?" the officer asked.

"That's right," Joe Ray answered again.

"And you gonna pay the money, anyhow?" the officer questioned.

"That's right!" Joe Ray repeated himself and handed the officer the money.

"You shore must be one honest feller."

"That's right!," came his reply the fourth time.

"It's a shame all that money got lost in the river. I bet its done washed down to the Atlantic Ocean by now, don't you?" the officer asked.

"You're right, again," Joe Ray agreed as he left the jail. Smiling, he headed back to where he had left Charlene.

The next day, he and Charlene were on their way to Atlanta. When they arrived at the Atlanta station, Joe Ray hoped to find his friend among the waiting carriage drivers, but such was not the case.

He summoned one of the drivers and instructed him to take them to the Magnolia Hotel on Peachtree Street.

"Do you know someone called Viney?" Joe Ray asked, as they stopped in front of their hotel.

"Yo' mean Driver Viney?" the black man answered. "Why, everyone in Atlanta knows Driver Viney, Sir. He's 'bout as well knowed as Mr. Lincoln."

"Then, will you tell him that Mr Franklin, from Dublin, requests his presence at this hotel tomorrow evening?" Joe Ray said, reaching the driver twice the amount of the fare.

"Most certainly, Sir," the driver answered, pleased at the amount Joe Ray gave him. "I'll see that he gits your message."

The next day was spent touring Atlanta. Charlene had become familiar with the city while she was in school, and was anxious to share her knowledge with Joe Ray.

Joe Ray was excited to learn, his only distraction being that of the passing carriages. Charlene could not help wondering why all the interest in one particular driver, but she did not question it, and Joe Ray was glad. He did not want her to know of the bond he had with his newly ac-quired friend.

It was late evening when the two arrived back at their hotel, and they were tired from the activities of the day. But, Joe Ray was uplifted to find Driver Viney waiting for him in the lobby.

Joe Ray opened his mouth as if to speak, but before he could do so, he was interrupted by Charlene.

"Excuse me," she said, as if sensing that the two men needed to be alone. "I believe I'll go on up and rest."

As soon as she disappeared at the top of the stairs, Joe Ray reached into his pocket and produced five new ten-dollar bills. "Here's the money I owe you," he said, and placed the bills into one of Driver Viney's calloused black hands. "And, were you serious about wanting to leave the city and live on a plantation?" he asked.

"More than anything on God's green earth," the old man replied.

"Then, have yourself and your missus at the station first thing Saturday morning, for that's just what you're going to do."

Tears appeared in the eyes of the white-haired old man, then slowly began flowing down the furrows life had so cruelly cut upon his face.

"How can I ever repay you, Sir?" he asked, both hands gently squeezing the hand of Joe Ray.

"You already have," answered Joe Ray, blinking hard so as not to reveal any sign of his own emotion. "You already have."

Joe Ray ascended the stairs, possessing a feeling of pride in what he had just accomplished. He had not known how much, moving to a plantation meant to Driver Viney, nor did Driver Viney know how much the money meant to him the day of his wedding, he reasoned.

"Wedding!" Joe Ray said to himself, loud enough for those around him to hear. He remembered that he still had not bought a ring for Charlene. That's what we'll do tomorrow, he thought, as he entered their room, eager to share his idea with his new bride.

Joe Ray and Charlene spent the following day shopping for the rings he had promised, but to his surprise, Charlene was of little help. She made it clear that the decision was his, and by evening, he realized she meant what she said. By dinner time, a decision was made and Charlene was the owner of a set of beautiful gold rings. That was harder than planting cotton, he thought, not daring to voice his opinion.

Anyway, all his business had been transacted, both in Macon and Atlanta, and he was looking forward to their return to the plantation.

Joe Ray and Charlene arrived at the station the following morning, just moments before their train was scheduled to depart Atlanta. They found Driver Viney and his wife, each seated on a large trunk near the ticket agent's stand. The trunks contained all their worldly possessions.

"We are here, jus' like I said we would be," he spoke, as Joe Ray approached. "An' this here, is my missus, Annie."

"An' you got to be Mr. Franklin's new wife," Annie said, addressing Charlene. "The Lord shore gonna bless you fer what you done," she continued. "We gonna make shore you won't never be sorry. My man been prayin' we would get back on a plantation ever since the war wuz over. He stayed up all night, 'cause he wuz so excited 'bout gettin' us out of the city."

"I'm sure we won't be," Charlene started to answer, but her voice was drowned out by the approaching train.

Joe Ray watched as their trunks were loaded onto the train and the Negro couple got aboard the car near the caboose.

By mid-afternoon, they were in Macon. He secured rooms for Charlene and himself, and found lodging nearby for Driver Viney and Annie.

"Its going to be good to be back home," he admitted to Charlene as they prepared for bed. "No wonder Driver Viney and his missus missed the peaceful life on the plantation. I can't see how anyone could give that up to live in the city."

"I don't either," Charlene replied. "Say, you never did tell me why we had to go on to Atlanta. Something you had to do, I recall."

"Why, I had to uh... I had to uh... buy your rings." he said, trying hard to think of any logical excuse.

"Certainly," Charlene yawned, snuggling a little closer to him. "Everyone knows they don't have any rings here in Macon."

The next day, as Charlene and Joe Ray stepped onto the platform at the Dublin station, Ole Ben was waiting.

"This is Driver Viney and Annie, his missus," Joe Ray said, introducing the Negro couple to Ole Ben. "From now on, they will live with us on the plantation."

"Not Driver Viney, anymore," the old man said, as he shook hands with Ole Ben. "Jus' Henry, from now on."

Strange, Joe Ray thought. Until now, I didn't know his name. He helped Old Ben load the trunks and waited until Driver Viney and his missus scooted themselves onto the back of the buggy.

"Is everybody ready to go?" Joe Ray asked, as he watched Henry remove his shoes, letting his feet dangle from the buggy, touching his feet to the sun-baked clay.

"We is now. I always knowed the Good Lord would put us back on the part of the earth where we belong." he said, smiling at Joe Ray.

As the buggy rolled along the road through the barren cotton fields, Henry became more excited.

"What's that cooking I smell?" he asked, even before the mansion and the old slave quarters came into view.

"Why, thats just a welcome home dinner Mattie and the others are fixin' up for Joe Ray and Miss Charlene," Ole Ben answered. "They wuz mighty let down 'cause they couldn't do it when yo' had your weddin', so they doin' it now."

"How nice, a welcome home celebration," Charlene said to Joe Ray.

And a celebration it was. For, when the mansion came into view, so did the half-grown pig that was roasting on a spit. The Negroes were dressed in their finest clothing, and a large table was filled with food fit for the President, himself.

As the buggy came to a stop, just short of where the table was prepared, everyone came running to welcome the newly married couple home. That is, everyone except Boss Bill. He, too, started toward the buggy, but turned and started racing up toward the mansion, as if someone had hollered 'FIRE!'"

Disregarding his father's actions, Joe Ray helped Charlene down from the buggy and started to introduce the new couple to the others.

"This is ..."

"Lordy! Lordy! Lordy! Dis is Henry an' my sister, Annie," Sara interrupted him, and went running to the back of the buggy. "I thought yo' wuz dead, many years back." she said, embracing the two new arrivals, hardly able to speak through her sobs of joy.

Joe Ray left Charlene to receive well wishes from Mattie and the others, and went to the mansion to find out what had drawn Boss Bill away so quickly.

As he entered the front door, he broke into uncontrollable laughter. Boss Bill had a sack and was grabbing money from everywhere.

"I wish you could move that fast when you were picking cotton," he said, still laughing so hard he could hardly speak.

"Don't just stand there brayin' like Luther's mule. Help me," Boss Bill said. Realizing how ridiculous he must look, Boss Bill also started laughing.

"I had to wait until all the furniture was put in here before I could hang the money to dry," he explained. "And in the middle of preparing for your welcome home celebration, I forgot to take it down. I didn't remember until the minute you arrived, and I was afraid Charlene and the others might see it."

Joe Ray helped Boss Bill collect the bills from the furniture, the stairways and the floors, and even from on the beds.   127

"Looks like Luther would have stolen bigger bills," Joe Ray said, as the last of the money was collected. "But, Luther never done anything that didn't cause more trouble," he added, still laughing.

"Where we gonna hide it, now?" Boss Bill asked.

"The same place I hid it before," Joe Ray answered. "Seems like as good a place as any, unless you want to hide it down in the well," he said, "so you can dry it again," and burst out laughing.

The rest of the day was filled with singing, dancing, and celebrating. By day's end, Charlene was made to feel as if she had always belonged there. The delivery and arranging of the furniture was a surprise far beyond her expectations.

Henry and Annie were comfortably settled in their quarters. Sara had seen to that, and the day of celebrating came to an end.

As Joe Ray and Charlene started up the rise to spend their first night in their own home, Sara appeared out of the shadows. "Good night, Mr. Joe Ray," she said, and squeezing Charlene, she added, "I knowed everthin' wuz gonna be alright."

The couple entered the mansion and walked up the spiral staircase leading to the sleeping quarters.

"Just a minute," Joe Ray said as he opened the door to Boss Bill's room. As he did, he could hear his father's even breathing and he knew he was enjoying peaceful sleep.

"I'm glad you decided your Daddy should have the room he once shared with your Mama," Charlene whispered.

128

"Me, too," Joe Ray answered, gently closing the door to Boss Bill's room. And as he took Charlene in his arms to carry her over the threshold, he added, "I think what Sara said is true. Everything is going to be alright."

"You'd best behave," Charlene whispered. "Its late and we have to get up early to go to Dublin for the reading of Daddy's will."

With one foot, he closed the door to their room.

"What do I need to go to Dublin for?" he asked. "I already got his most valuable possession."

Chapter Thirteen
The Will

Joe Ray and Charlene were not disturbed until almost mid-morning. A gentle knock on the bedroom door awakened them at almost the same time. Charlene sat up in bed and took a moment to reacquaint herself with the surroundings.

"Who's there?" she finally asked, as if she were afraid it might be some strange intruder.

"Its only me and Annie," Sara answered, as both ladies entered the room, each bearing a large covered tray. "Mattie done let us know that she wuz boss in that bran' new kitchen, and she done give us orders to bring these platters up to yo're room."

"And, what are to be your chores?" Charlene asked of Sara and Annie.

"Mattie said she s'posed our job would be to keep dis place lookin' as shiny an' new as it do right now." Sara answered.

"And what do you think of those arrangements?" Charlene questioned.

"We'd be mos' proud to," said Sara.

"An' keep it shiny, we will," Annie added.

"Then, that's the way it shall be done." Charlene stated, uncovering the trays that sat before them.

"Are you going to have one of these, or am I going to eat both trays myself?" Charlene asked Joe Ray.

Sitting up in bed, eyeing the delicious breakfast, he teased, "I'll eat them both, myself. Want Sara to bring you something?"

"Then, you'd better hurry," Charlene replied. "It will soon be time to go to Dublin. Today is the reading of Daddy's will."

"I'm sure glad your Daddy didn't know about our marriage," Joe Ray said, as he finished the last mouthful of his breakfast. "Or, there would be no need of your being present at the reading of his will."

"You're probably right," Charlene agreed, "but, as things are, we might be rich."

"Then, let's hurry, so we can find out," Joe Ray said, still teasing her.

When at last, they were ready to leave, Ole Ben was waiting.

They arrived at Lawyer William McCord's office ahead of the others. The lawyer greeted them as they came into his office. "Why, you must be Miss Charlene McClanahan, John's only daughter. I ain't seen you since you were this big."

"Charlene Franklin," Charlene interrupted, "and this is my husband, Joe Ray. And, yes, I am Mr. McClanahan's only daughter."

"Your husband?" the lawyer asked, unable to control his surprise. "How long you been married, Miss McClanahan, I mean Mrs. Franklin?" he asked.

"Three whole weeks, now," she answered. "But, why do you ask?"

"Oh, no reason," he said, shaking his head in disbelief. "Just funny how some marriages cost so much more than others. Just have a seat and we'll get started as soon as the others arrive."

Joe Ray and Charlene spent the next few minutes trying to figure our what McCord meant.

"How does he know what our wedding cost?" Joe Ray asked, "and what business is it of his, anyway?"

In a little while, all the McClanahans made their way into the office. The lawyer met them as they entered and expressed his sympathy, then, escorted everyone into a larger room.

When they were all seated around a huge table, which was the only furniture in the room, the lawyer began to speak.

"Today, we are here to carry out the wishes of one of my oldest and dearest friends. It was his desire that I read and execute the requirements set forth in this, his will."

With that, he extracted some papers from a leather

case that lay in front of him. He cleared his throat and began to read.

I, John Thomas McClanahan, of Warren County, Georgia, being of sound mind and disposing memory, do hereby make, publish , and declare this to be my Last Will and Testament, hereby revoking any and all wills by me at anytime, heretofore made.

First: I direct that all my debts be paid.

Second: I give, devise, and bequeath all my real estate to my four sons, except that which was once part of the Franklin plantation, providing they allow their mother to continue residence on said property for the duration of her remaining years.

Third: I give, devise, and bequeath to each of my sons the sum of twenty-five thousand dollars (25,000).

Fourth: I give, devise, and bequeath to each of my former slaves who still remain on the plantation at the time of this reading, the sum of two thousand dollars (2,000).

Fifth: I give, devise, and bequeath to my only daughter, Charlene, all the acreage which was once part of the Franklin plantation, and the sum of ten thousand dollars (10,000), providing she does not marry before her twenty-first birthday. In the event she has taken unto her a husband, she is to receive only the money. The aforesaid real estate shall be sold immediately at public auction, the proceeds of which I bequeath to her mother.

If this seems cruel, my dear Charlene, it is only to allow you time to find someone to whom you are better suited and forget the one with whom you have been keeping company.

Sixth: I give, devise, and bequeath all my personal property, including the remainder of my monetary holdings to my beloved wife, Charlotte McClanahan.

Seventh: I hereby nominate and appoint my attorney, William McCord, to be executor of this my last will and testament.

Given under my hand and seal, this, the 26th day of April, 1876.

The lawyer folded the papers from which he had been reading.

Turning to Charlene, he said, "Now, you understand what I meant by some marriages costing more than others. By your own admission," he added, "I have determined that you are already married, a marriage your dear, departed father tried desperately to prevent. You understand, of course, that the property must be sold."

"I understand," Charlene answered, trying hard not to let her anger and frustration show. She ran from the office without further comment.

"How could he be so cruel?" she asked, as Joe Ray followed her out of the building. "No one should have that much control over another."

"I must advertise the sale of the property for thirty days prior to the auction," they heard McCord say, as the others came filing out of the office.

"I will begin proceedings at once. And since I'm sure there are no debts owing, having handled the affairs of your father for many years, I will have drafts drawn up for each of the heirs right away," directing his comments to her brothers, sensing her mother was in no state of mind to comprehend anything that was being said.

"Looks like Daddy knew exactly what he was doing," commented Charlene's oldest brother, Bobby. "He may not have won the war, but he won most of the battles."

"Let's be going," she said to Joe Ray, as Ole Ben drove the carriage to where they were waiting. "Before I forget I am a lady," she added.

"I'm truly sorry," Joe Ray told her as they drove away. "If we had only known, we could have waited."

"Don't you ever say you're sorry for marrying me, Joe Ray Franklin," Charlene could no longer hide her anger. "The only thing I'm sorry about is that Daddy died before he knew we were married."

Chapter Fourteen
The Sale

As the day of the auction drew nearer, more and more people came to look over the land that was to be sold. Since the property line was so close to where they lived, many of the inquiries about the sale were directed at Boss Bill and Joe Ray.

There were questions like: "How much you think it'll bring?" "How many bales of cotton will it grow?" "Does it have any buildings?" And the questions went on and on.

There were even rumors that buyers from New York were going to purchase the land and build textile mills. After all, they could manufacture finished products right here in the heart of the cotton fields and thus, eliminate the shipping costs to their mills up north.

"I hope how quick this thing is over with," Joe Ray told Charlene, on the evening prior to the sale.

"Me, too," she agreed. "I only wish we could buy the land, then, your father's plantation would once again be like it was before the war. With the mansion as good as it ever was, and if we could buy the land, everything would be just like when we were small."

"Do you mean that, Charlene?" Joe Ray asked, as he began to tabulate what the cost might be. "Wouldn't it be wonderful if we could buy Daddy's land back and have the plantation like it used to be?"

"I'd like that more than anything," Charlene answered.

"Then, let's do it," Joe Ray yelled, jumping from the mansion step, grabbing Charlene's hand, half dragging her onto the lawn.

"How in thunder can we afford to buy the land?" Charlene asked. "And where are we going in such a hurry? Joe Ray, I think you have taken leave of your senses," she told him.

But Joe Ray did not slow down until they reached the old barn at the far end of the row of shacks.

"With this," he told her as he opened the grain box, revealing the money hidden inside.

"Where in the world did you get that?" Charlene questioned. "How much is there?"

"I don't know," Joe Ray answered. "Can you keep a secret?"

Charlene shook her head, indicating that she could, and at the same time looked around to make sure no one else was present.

"Then, I'll tell you," Joe Ray began.

He told Charlene how he came upon Luther in the act of robbing the train, and how he later found the money.

"And you don't know how much you have?" she questioned.

"No," Joe Ray replied. "The rumor is that there is over a hundred thousand."

"Then, let's go count it," Charlene squeaked, pulling the sack of money from the grain box.

Charlene and Joe Ray took the money to the privacy of their bedroom and began counting.

"Hundred one, hundred two, hundred three, hundred four. There's a hundred and four stacks, and each of them has a thousand in it," Charlene said, when they finished counting.

"That's a hundred and four thousand dollars," Joe Ray said. "You sure they all got a thousand in them?"

"All except this one," Charlene teased, stuffing some bills down the front of her low-cut dress. "This is for shopping. I'm going to buy some new clothes, and I'm going to buy Mattie, Sara, and Annie a new bonnet."

"And me a new fishing pole," Joe Ray added.

"What do you need a new fishing pole for?" questioned Charlene.

"So I can go down to the river and see if old Luther tried to hold out any of that money," he laughed.

"Two fishing poles, then," Charlene told him, throwing a handful of money into the air, letting it shower down upon them.

The next morning, Joe Ray and Charlene were up early. They woke Boss Bill and told him of their plans.

"You just might pull it off," Joe Ray's father told them, as he started to figure. "Let's see, now," he said, "we got some money left from the sale of the cotton, and Luther loaned us over a hundred thousand dollars."

"And I got the ten thousand Daddy left me," Charlene volunteered.

"Yeah, you might just pull it off," Boss Bill smiled. "Remember, Joe Ray," he added, "I told you that the south might rise again."

By mid-morning on the day of the sale, crowds of people could be seen gathering on the land that was to be auctioned, although the sale wasn't to begin until exactly noon.

· "We might as well go visit some of the local people," Boss Bill urged, anxious to get started.

"Fine with me," Joe Ray said as he, Charlene and Boss Bill climbed into their buggy.

When they approached the crowd, they encountered many familiar faces. Auctions always brought people from far and wide, and this one had drawn almost everyone in the county. People were everywhere, both black and white. Some of them came to visit neighbors they had not seen since the last gathering of this nature. Some came just to be nosy, and others came, hoping to win one of the few silver dollars they knew would be given away. And a few even came, hoping to buy. For whatever reason, the crowd was getting larger, and in a matter of minutes, the bidding would begin. 140

Joe Ray and Boss Bill left Charlene in the buggy with Ole Ben and were visiting some neighbors a short distance away.

"And this is Mr. McClanahan's daughter," Lawyer McCord said, as he introduced Charlene to a well-dressed gentlemen that Joe Ray had never seen before.

"This is Mr. Daniels," McCord continued. "I have brought him all the way from Macon to conduct this sale. His reputation is that of being the best auctioneer in the whole state of Georgia."

"Pleased to meet you, Miss McClanahan," came the booming voice from the man to whom she had been introduced.

"No, it's Mrs. Franklin," Charlene started to correct, but was interrupted by the booming voice before she could finish.

"It's high noon and time to get started," the voice was saying.

"No wonder he is supposed to be so good," Charlene thought. "With a voice like that, he could be heard in any size crowd, even in the midst of a thunderstorm."

"Time to get started," he said once again, and the crowd began to quiet down.

Joe Ray and Boss Bill moved back along the side of the buggy as the auctioneer described the boundaries of the property that was about to be sold.

"Are there any questions?" the loud voice asked. He hesitated for just a moment, then shouted. "Then, let the bidding begin!"

"Twenty thousand dollars," yelled someone from near the stand that had been built for the auctioneer.

"Twenty thousand, and we're off," the auctioneer boomed. "Bid by Mr. Sutton, the gentleman from New York."

Joe Ray was glad their buggy was in back of the crowd. That way, they could see better, who was doing the bidding.

"Twenty-five," it was Charlene's older brother, Bobby, who submitted the second bid.

"Twenty-five," the auctioneer repeated, "bid by Mr. McClanahan. And now, do I hear thirty?"

"Thirty," came a voice from someone further back in the crowd.

"Thirty," the auctioneer boomed, "from Mr. Smith from Boston.

"Thirty-five," again, it was the buyer from New York.

"Forty," this time it was Billy, Charlene's youngest brother, who was standing only a few feet in front of them.

"Forty, McClanahan," the auctioneer repeated.

"Fifty," came another bid.

"Fifty, Mr Smith," said the auctioneer.

Joe Ray could tell by the recognition given to each of the bidders that the auctioneer had met Charlene's brothers and most of the other potential buyers. Perhaps they had purchased property at other auctions he had conducted.

"Fifty-five," again. It was Sutton, the gentleman from New York.

"Sixty," again. It was Bobby.

142

"Sixty, McClanahan. Do I hear sixty-five?"

"Sixty-five." It was the gentleman from Boston, again.

"Seventy." Billy raised his hand, indicating to the auctioneer.

"Seventy-five." Sutton did the bidding this time.

"Seventy-five, Sutton," the auctioneer boomed even louder. "Seventy-five, and now eighty, eighty, eighty. Do I hear eighty?"

"Eighty thousand." It was Bobby this time.

"Eighty-thousand dollars," the auctioneer repeated. "Do I hear more? I have eighty thousand dollars from Mr. McClanahan. Do I hear eighty-five?"

"What you say?" he asked Mr Sutton, the man from New York.

"I'm through," the New Yorker replied.

"Eighty-one, thank you, sir," the auctioneer said to the Boston bidder. "And now, do I hear eighty-two?"

"Now," Boss Bill said to Charlene in a low voice, indicating it was time for her to bid.

"Do I hear eighty-two? the auctioneer was asking, seeming to know the bidding was slowing down. "Do I hear eighty-two?"

Charlene raised her hand, gesturing her bid of eighty-two thousand.

Acknowledging her bid, the auctioneer moved on. "And now, eighty two, I have eighty-two from McClanahan. And now, I need eighty-three. Eighty-three, eighty-three. What about it, Mr Smith, do I hear eighty-three?"

"My firm has only authorized me to go as high as eighty-one thousand," he said. "And it appears that figure is not high enough."

"Then, I have eighty-two, eighty-two, eighty-two. Do I hear eighty-three? I have eighty-two, McClanahan. And now, do I hear eighty-three?

The auctioneer asked for eighty-three thousand several more times, but no other bids were offered.

Each of Charlene's brothers, thinking the other had submitted the last bid, made no other attempt at bidding.

"Eighty-two once, eighty-two twice, eighty-two thousand dollars, sold to Miss McClanahan," the auctioneer said as he lowered his gavel, signaling the bidding was over.

"That's Mrs Franklin, Mrs. Joe Ray Franklin," Charlene yelled loud enough for everyone in the crowd to hear, as she threw herself from the buggy into Joe Ray's arms.

"She can't pay," screamed her older brother. "She don't have the money. She can't pay eighty-two thousand dollars."

"You understand that the amount you have bid must be delivered in full to Mr. McCord's office Friday morning, Miss McClanahan, I mean Mrs. Franklin?" the auctioneer asked Charlene.

"Should I bring a draft, or will cash be alright? Charlene asked in a businesslike manner.

"Cash will be fine, I'm sure," boomed the auctioneer's voice once more.

"I'll bet he couldn't whisper if his life depended on

it," Charlene giggled, squeezing Joe Ray a little tighter.

"How in the world do you expect to come up with that kind of money?" one of her brothers asked, as all four strolled up to the buggy.

"Oh, I guess we'll have to use some of Joe Ray's inheritance," she said mockingly, as she, Joe Ray and Boss Bill climbed back into the buggy.

"What inheritance?" her older brother asked, as Ole Ben started to drive away.

"You wouldn't believe it, anyway," Joe Ray interjected. "And furthermore," he added, "your Daddy didn't win most of the battles, he just died before the war was over."

"Let's get back to the plantation," he instructed Ole Ben.

Ole Ben brought the horse to a complete stop.

"What's wrong?" Joe Ray questioned.

"Iffen yo' plantation is where yo' wants to go, Mr. Joe Ray, sir, yo' already there."

"He's exactly right," Charlene began laughing, as the others joined in. "But, let's go, so we can tell the others."

On Sunday evening, following the auction, Joe Ray, Charlene and Boss Bill were lounging on the mansion lawn. They were joined by Mattie, Ole Ben, Sara, Annie, Driver Viney and the others who lived on the plantation.

Everyone was talking of the happenings of the past season and the good fortune they expected in the coming year.

"I guess you'll have to hire more help as soon as the new quarters are completed," Joe Ray told Boss Bill. "Cause next year, we're gonna raise more cotton than we did before the war."

"An' I ain't gonna help yo', neither," Ole Ben said smiling. "I'm gonna be takin' care of dem new horses we gonna be buyin'"

"We ain't helpin' neither," Sara said. "Me an' sister Annie gonna be busy keepin' dis mansion house nice an' shiny."

"Don' figger I be helpin' neither," said Mattie, as she took another piece of chicken and another biscuit from the basket she had prepared for all to enjoy. "It say right heah in de Good Book," pointing to the open Bible lying in her lap, "dat yo' should earn yo' bread by de sweat of yo' brow, an' I shore druther be sweatin' up there in dat brand new kitchen, than out there in dem cotton fields."

"Since I ain't got no health good enough to 'low me to work in the cotton, neither, I guess I might as well just go find me a good place for my buryin'," Henry said. "Dat's what I come back to the plantation country fo' anyhow, so I could be buried in the cotton fields."

"How soon you planning on dying, anyway?" Boss Bill asked.

"Probably quick as he eats dem other seben pieces of Mattie's chicken," Annie joked.

"It also say heah, dat yo' don' have to worry 'bout gettin' even wif nobody," Mattie said, referring once again to her Bible. "It say heah dat de Lord said, 'Vengeance is Mine.'"

Remembering how hard her daddy tried to keep them

146

apart, Joe Ray smiled, pulling Charlene a little closer to his side. "I sure do like your reading from the Good Book, Mattie. Especially, them last three words, 'Vengeange is Mine.'"

Mattie hesitated for several moments. "I 'spose things works out like dey's meant to be," she said, more to herself than to anyone else. "I'se can make sense 'bout how de Good Lord would want yo' to get yo're land back, Joe Ray, an' I'se can see how He would want yo' an' Miss Charlene to git married, 'cause yo' shore do make a fine pair. But, I'se ain't never gonna know why He ever put de notion in Luther's head to go rob dat train."

"Because," Charlene replied, "I guess, like it says there in your Good Book, He does work in mysterious ways."

Chapter Fifteen
Return To Atlanta

The passing of time always brings about many changes. Life on the Franklin Plantation was no exception. The next two years was a time of adjustment, not only for Joe Ray, but for everyone who lived on the land they had cherished most of their lives.

Joe Ray was at last, enjoying the lifestyle he heard his father and the former slaves talk about during the many times they congregated outside the old shack that he and Boss Bill called home. He now fully understood why his father was so devastated by having seen nearly everything, he and his mother spent a lifetime building, torn apart. He could also understand why the shock of being reduced to poverty, after having enjoyed such a life of leisure, had brought on the death of his mother.

Boss Bill, once again, resumed the task of making

sure the cotton fields were planted and harvested as he had done during the years prior to the war. This was a simple job now, for everyone who remained on the land, was more than anxious to do whatever they could to help in order to show their appreciation. The old run-down slave shacks were torn down and new living quarters built to accommodate each of the Negro families.

Life for Charlene was little different than what she enjoyed while living at home. Mattie, Sara, and Mrs. Viney made sure that the mansion was kept spotless and their meals were ready on time. Driver Viney, Henry, to everyone now, took charge of seeing that the grounds surrounding the mansion were well-kept and the vegetable and flower gardens were second to none in the South.

Charlene rarely visited the plantation where she grew up. Within a fortnight of her father being killed, her mother also passed away, leaving only her brothers to carry out the duties of managing the McClanahan holdings. Her three younger brothers held no resentment toward Charlene for having married Joe Ray and made her welcome each time she visited. They seemed happy for their little sister and Joe Ray, pleased that the war had not done to her, what it had done to their mother. Bobby, on the other hand, still harbored all the hatred toward the Franklins, that was passed down to him by his father.

Shortly after the death of his mother, Bobby moved to Atlanta and bought a hardware store. He grew tired of life on his family's plantation and set out to start a new life in the city. He also wanted to remove himself from any

150

dealings with the Franklins, or having anything to do with Charlene, whom he felt, brought shame and embarassment to the entire McClanahan family.

He knew that by moving to Atlanta, he would be far enough away, that he would no longer have to deal with the situation in which Charlene had placed him. He also knew that due to the fact that so many northerners were coming south to start up textile mills and other manufacturing facilities, owning a hardware store would be a very profitable business. Thus, he invested the money his father left him and began a new life in Atlanta, where he knew he would have no dealings with Charlene or anyone else from the Franklin Plantation.

Most evenings at the Franklin home were spent lounging on the front lawn. After the evening meal, Joe Ray, Charlene and Boss Bill returned to the front porch of the mansion. Some of the Negro folks would usually be waiting for them by the time the three of them arrived, and Mattie, Sara, and Mrs. Viney would join them after the kitchen was cleaned and everything put in its proper place.

The Franklins never separated themselves from any of the others or gave any indication of being their superior. Everyone was treated equally, regardless of color, and each one was made to feel that they were part of the family.

Each evening, the conversation among the group was much like that of the days before. They talked of the hardships the war had brought and how working together, they had overcome, and were enjoying life better than any of them thought it could be.

Many times, Charlene spoke of Bobby. She felt that somehow, she needed to find him and try to make him understand that marrying Joe Ray was in no way meant to embarrass the family. As far as she knew, her older brother had no contact with anyone in her family since he left the plantation. She did not know his whereabouts, nor did she know anyone who knew what was going on in his life. She only knew, that to make peace with Bobby, was going to be one of her goals.

Also, Luther was usually one of the topics the group often discussed. No one knew if his body had ever been found somewhere down-river, or if he truly had washed into the Atlantic Ocean. Joe Ray knew well, that if it had not been for Luther and his daring train robbery, life for his family would be nowhere near what they now enjoyed. He missed the good times he and Luther shared, especially the times the two of them spent fishng from the banks of the Oconee River. He did, however, hold a morsel of resentment toward him for stealing the letters Charlene sent while she was away in Atlanta.

Ole Ben and Mattie also spoke often of Luther and wished they could know how his life ended, but found consolation in believing their Creator would find enough good in Luther to allow him into Heaven. Neither of them knew what happened to the money their son had taken, but they felt that because of the hardships the slaves had to endure, that God reserved a special place for them in His Kingdom. This thought kept them from worrying about their son after he entered the great beyond.

Nightfall was drawing nigh and some of the Negroes were beginning to slip away to their separate places of abode, when the sound of an approaching carriage was heard. Everyone waited to see who could be coming to visit at this late hour. In a few moments, the carriage pulled onto the lawn and the driver inquired as to the whereabouts of one Mrs. Joe Ray Franklin.

"This is Mrs. Franklin," Joe Ray said, pointing in the direction of Charlene.

"Then, I have a message for you," the driver stated and extracted a folded piece of paper from his inside coat pocket.

Charlene thanked the driver and unfolded the message and began to read. She finished and refolded the message. Turning to Joe Ray, she relayed the content of what she had read.

"There has been a terrible accident," she said. "Bobby is in a hospital in Atlanta and is not expected to live. The message indicates that he wishes to see the both of us as soon as possible."

"Then, we will leave first thing in the morning," Joe Ray said. "Henry, will you be ready to take us to Dublin at first light?"

The next day was hectic for everyone on the plantation. They knew how Charlene wanted to know the whereabouts of her oldest brother and were relieved that she had learned where he was, but they also shared her grief.

Joe Ray and Charlene barely reached the bottom step of the mansion, when Henry pulled up in the buggy.

"If we loose no time, we can catch the morning train to Macon," Joe Ray instructed the driver. "Then, we can get the noon train on to Atlanta. With any luck at all, we should reach our destination by nightfall."

And so it was. Joe Ray and Charlene arrived in Atlanta just as daylight gave way to darkness. As they stepped from the train, rain was beginning to fall. There were two buggies waiting near the station platform to deliver the arriving passengers to wherever they wanted to go. Joe Ray signaled to one of the drivers and waited for him to pull up where he and Charlene were standing. By the time the buggy reached the couple, the rain really started to pour down. Joe Ray helped Charlene into the buggy, paying little attention to the driver, except for the fact, he seemed to have a crippled arm.

"To the Magnolia Hotel," Joe Ray instructed him. "And, do you know the location of the hospital here in Atlanta?" he asked.

"Shore do, sir," was the driver's reply.

"Then, pick us up at eight o'clock tomorrow morning and take us to the hospital," Joe Ray said. "How much is the fare for tonight?" he asked.

"Rainin' too hard to talk 'bout fares tonight," the driver stated. "I'se jus' put it on what yo's goin' to owe me in de mornin', iffen dat be alright wif yo'?"

Joe Ray shot a puzzling look at the driver. He was sitting on the buggy seat with the rain dripping from the hat he was wearing. His beard looked as if someone had hit him in the face with a bucket of water.

154

"Fair enough to me," Joe Ray answered as he helped Charlene from the buggy.

"Something sure seems familiar about that driver," Joe Ray thought, as he ushered Charlene to the front desk of the hotel.

The couple got very little sleep that night. Most of their time was discussing how long Bobby had lived in Atlanta, and what sort of accident he could have been involved in.

The next morning, the buggy driver was waiting in front of the hotel as he had been instructed. As Joe Ray helped Charlene aboard, he noticed a crutch, leaning on the driver's seat.

"Something about our driver puzzles me, Charlene," he stated as the driver moved the buggy onto the cobblestone street and headed toward the hospital. "Seems like I've seen him before," he continued, "but, that can't be. I don't know a soul in Atlanta, except your brother, Bobby, and I didn't even know he was in Atlanta."

Nothing else was said during the fifteen or twenty-minute drive to the hospital. Both, Joe Ray's and Charlene's thoughts were on what had happened to her brother.

In a little while, they reached their destination. Joe Ray could see a sign painted on the front of one of the largest buildings in the city.

"How much for last night and this morning," Joe Ray started to ask as he approached the driver.

"Free ride both times, Joe Ray," the driver answered.

Taken aback and startled that the driver knew his

155

name, Joe Ray looked up at the black man on the buggy seat.

"Luther! You lazy, horse stealing, lying excuse for humanity! I thought you was dead. Everybody thought you was dead."

"Don't be talking so loud," Luther almost whispered. "My name ain't Luther no more. It's Lucas. Driver Lucas, mos' folks 'round 'Lanta knows me by. An' as fer bein' dead, only some parts of me is dead. Dat be one arm an' de better part of one leg."

"I'm shore glad you're not dead, Luther." Joe Ray continued, "Now, I can kill you, myself, for what you did with Charlene's letters."

"It's Lucas," Luther corrected. "Yo' gonna git me hung iffen yo' don' quit callin' me dat other feller's name."

"I can think of a lot of names I'd like to call you, but I don't have time to call you anything, now, Luther. Me and Charlene are here to visit her brother, Bobby. I want you to wait right here on us until we are ready to go back to our hotel. And then, me and you are going to have us a long talk." Joe Ray continued, "If you don't wait on us, I will tell every lawman in Atlanta who you really are."

"I'll be right heah, jus' like yo' wants me to be," Luther answered. "An', by the way, how's ole Sadie Mae?"

"Your mule is just like you, Luther, I mean Lucas, just as hard-headed as she ever was. Now, you stay here and wait for us."

Joe Ray left Luther pondering what he said, concerning the law and accompanied Charlene into the hospital.

156

Inside the hospital, the couple were greeted by a dignified-looking lady, whom they assumed, must be a nurse.

"We are here to see my brother, Bobby, I mean Robert McClanahan," Charlene told her. " I understand he has been hurt in some sort of accident."

"Of course," the lady replied. "And you must be Charlene. Your brother has instructed everyone here, that you are to be brought to his room immediately upon your arrival. Please have a seat," she instructed, pointing to one corner that contained a few large chairs. "I will take you to your brother's room directly. But, I'm sure the doctor will talk to you, first."

The nurse left the room and in minutes, returned with a gentlemen whom she introduced as Dr. John Henley.

"I am one of the doctors attending to your brother," he said to Charlene.

"This is my husband, Joe Ray Franklin," Charlene answered. "What happened to Bobby?" she asked.

"Seems Mr. McClanahan lived in back of the hardware store he owns. He apparently fell asleep at his desk a few nights ago, while working on the day's receipts. As far as anyone can determine, he must have left a candle burning, which caught his hardware store on fire."

"Anyway," the doctor continued, "your brother has severe burns over a large area of his body and we have been unable to control the infection. I regret to inform you, Mrs. Franklin, but it looks as if your brother will not survive. His burns are the worst I have ever encountered, even when treating our soldiers during the war. I surmise that seeing you is the only thing that has allowed him to live this long."

"Thank you, Dr. Henley," was Charlene's reply. "May we see him, now?"

"Yes, but for only a short while. He is growing weaker with each passing hour and I must warn you, he is in severe pain, in spite of all the medication."

A nurse ushered Joe Ray and Charlene to her brother's room. "Your sister is here to see you, sir," she said to Bobby. "I will leave you to visit, now."

"Thank you for coming," Bobby spoke in a voice that was weak and almost unrecognizable. "The doctors tell me that I will not be able to overcome what has happened to me."

He continued, "I cannot depart this life without making peace with you. The truth of the matter is that our father always thought he would be the one to marry your mother," he said to Joe Ray. "When your daddy stole her from him, his hatred toward Mr. Franklin began, and now, I am sorry to say, only grew worse as time passed."

"You are in no condition to talk, now," Charlene interrupted. "You must rest now, and we can talk later."

"No," Bobby went on, in a voice that was growing weaker. "I am sorry for the way I have treated Joe Ray and I want to make it up to you in the only way I know how. I am getting very tired, now, but I want you to promise that you will return later today and bring a lawyer with you."

Charlene could tell that her brother was indeed, very tired and finding it more difficult to hide his pain.

"Whatever you wish," Charlene answered. "But,

you're going to be as good as new. Just you wait and see."

"Please. Just do as I ask," Bobby stated.

"Then, we shall see you later today," Charlene said as she and Joe Ray left the room.

"Where are we going to find a lawyer?" she asked, trying not to show the grief that was tearing her apart.

"We'll leave that up to Luther," Joe Ray answered. "That is, if he hasn't hightailed it out of Atlanta by now."

Just as he promised, Luther was right where the couple had left him earlier.

"Take us to a lawyer's office," Joe Ray instructed, as he helped Charlene aboard the buggy.

"What yo' want to see a lawyer fer?" Luther questioned nervously. "Yo' ain't gonna tell de lawmen 'bout me, are you?"

"No!" came Joe Ray's answer. "This has to do with another matter, and besides, I'm going to deal with you all by myself. Now, take us to see that lawyer."

"Which one of dem lawyers yo' wants to see?" Luther asked. "There's more lawyers in "Lanta than dey is black folks, since all de northern folks started movin' down heah."

"Any one of them you wish," Joe Ray scolded. "Let's get going."

Joe Ray and Charlene had no trouble finding a lawyer who was willing to meet them at the hospital later that day, although they knew nothing about what Bobby had in mind. Four o'clock was the hour both parties agreed to meet, leaving Joe Ray ample time to deal with his long-lost friend.

"Back to the hotel, driver," Joe Ray commanded, as

they left the lawyer's office. "And, what time is it now?"

"Zakly 'leven-thirty," Luther responded.

"Very good. Give us one hour to have lunch in the hotel diner, and then, come up to our room. You and I are going to have us a man to man talk, Luther."

"Up stairs, last door on the left," Joe Ray added.

At exactly half past the noon hour, there was a knock at the Franklins' hotel room door.

"Come in, Luther," Joe Ray invited. "At least you have learned to tell time even if you haven't learned to do much else."

Luther hobbled into the room and took a seat near the only window in the room. Joe Ray could tell that he looked much older than he knew him to be.

"What have you been doing for the past two years?" Joe Ray began to question. "I know you been doing something besides robbing trains. You already proved that you aren't very good at that line of work."

"I been drivin' folks 'round the city mos' all time I been in 'Lanta," Luther answered. "I been makin' good money doin' it, too, iffen I do say so, mysef."

"How did you ever get up here in Atlanta?" Joe Ray questioned. "And, how did you ever come to start driving a buggy? Everyone in Dublin thought you must be somewhere in the Atlantic Ocean."

"Well, hits like dis," Luther began, looking in the direction of Charlene as if she knew nothing of his past. "When I took de money offin' dat train, one of dem guards shot me clean through de shoulder an' made me loose dat whole sack

160

of cash in de river. I wuz hurtin' some kind of real bad, but I kept mysef live 'til I wash't a mile down de river.

De nex' day, I jumped on de train goin' up to Macon an' I kept on ridin' hit 'til I got to 'Lanta. Dat's where I got offin de train, 'cause I wuz hurtin' so bad. I knowed I couldn't ride no more. I crawled to de horse stables an' stayed 'til nex' mornin'. Dat's where one of de buggy drivers named, Henry, fount me. When he axed me what happened, I tol' him I looked like a feller dat had been cheatin' in a poker game down in Macon an' one of de loosers shot me 'fore he knowed I wuz de wrong feller."

"Then, what happened?" Joe Ray asked.

"Dat's when Driver Viney started feelin' sorry fer me, I reckon, an' took me to where him an' his missus lived."

When Luther mentioned Henry Viney, Charlene started to speak for the first time since their guest entered the room. Lucky for Joe Ray, Luther didn't notice when he placed a finger to his lips, indicating for her to keep silent.

"Dey wuz real good to me," Luther continued. "Dey give me food to eat an' Missus Viney took care of my shoulder, de one dat been shot."

"Then, what?" Joe Ray wanted to know.

"Den, one night, Mr. Henry come home talkin' like he was plum crazy, sayin' stuff like, he done met some feller frum way down on dem plantations close to where he growed up 'fore de war. He told his missus to start gittin' their blongin's together, 'cause dey wuz leavin' de nex' morning an' dey wuzn't never comin' back to de city.

Mr. Henry said I wuz gittin' better 'nough to drive,

161

so I could have his horse and buggy. An' I could even stay on at de boardin' house where he lived iffen it wuz alright wif de ones dat owned it. So, rite heah, is where I'se been ever since. I guess Mr. Henry must not'a been crazy as I thought, 'cause I ain't seen nor heard of him after dat."

"So, what happened to your leg?" Joe Ray asked, staring at the crutch Luther laid on the floor beside where he was sitting.

"Oh, dey ain't nothin' matter of my leg," Luther grinned. "I jus' fount dis crutch de day after Mr. Henry left, so I didn't won' hit to go to waste. 'Sides, now, when I'se outside where folks can see me, I pertend like I'm crippled. An' when dey wants to know what happened to me, I jus' say I'se born dis way. Dat way, none of 'em knows who I really is."

"Suppose that's why you let your beard grow, too," Joe Ray said.

"Shore 'nough," was luther's response. "An' it does good, too. 'Cause ain't nobody ever knowed who I really wuz, up 'til now."

"What about those railroad guards?" Joe Ray continued. "What if one on them had recognized you?"

"Dat don't bother me none, neither, Joe Ray. I done hauled de one dat shot me ten or more times an' he ain't got no notion hit's me dat robbed dat train. I'se been doin' good, heah in 'Lanta, but I shore would like to be back home, so me and yo' could go back fishin'" Luther added. "I ain't been fishin' fer past two years, now, an' I shore would like to have me a mess of dem catfish. Som'times I can almos'

162

taste catfish, I like 'em so good. Anyhow, is my mama an' daddy doin' alright?"

"They are both doing real well and very happy, too," Joe Ray answered. "I wondered why you asked about your mule earlier and didn't even mention your folks."

Luther hesitated for a moment before speaking. "'Cause I wuz 'fraid yo' might tell me dey wuz already dead," he stammered.

"Why did you keep Charlene's letters hidden from me?" Joe Ray questioned, not even trying to hide his frustration.

"'Cause I knowed iffen yo' an' Miss Charlene kept writin' dem letters all de time, yo' would end up gittin' married an' maybe start raisin' a bunch of young'uns. Den, me an' yo' would never have no time to go fishin' or ever go to Macon."

"Is fishin' all you ever think about, Luther?"

"Mos' times," Luther stated and then, turning to Charlene, he added, "I'se real sorry fo' what I done, Miss Charlene."

Joe Ray started to make another comment, but Charlene interrupted. "It's time for us to get back to the hospital if we are going to meet the lawyer at four o'clock."

"Get the buggy, Luther," Joe Ray instructed.

Luther got up without hesitation and quickly started for the door, glad that the conversation about the letters had ended.

"Better take this crutch," Joe Ray reminded him. "Someone might get the idea you weren't born as bad off as

163

you been letting on."

"Shore 'nough," Luther grinned. He took the crutch from Joe Ray and was out the door.

"I'm going to take that lying black boy back to Dublin with us," he said to Charlene as they exited their room. "Ole Ben and Miss Mattie will be glad to know he's still alive. And If I don't, he'll end up getting himself hung for stealing half the city of Atlanta."

When the couple reached the hospital, the lawyer had already arrived. They made their way to Bobby's room, only to find him in a much worse condition than when they left just a few hours earlier.

"We have a lawyer, as you requested," Charlene spoke in a tone that was almost a whisper.

"Good. Have him write down what I am about to say," Bobby stated, trying as best he could, to hide the pain.

"Because you and Joe Ray were already married at the time of Daddy's death, the income from the sale of the property that was once part of the Franklin estate, was left to our mother. Since she died shortly after our daddy was buried, her holdings were left to their five children. As administrator of the estate, I deposited your share in the bank in Dublin, without you knowing what had happened. I also deposited the portion that was left to me. This money, I now leave to you and Joe Ray, as I will no longer have need of it. Can you have this paper drawn up immediately?" he asked, looking in the direction of the lawyer.

"Within the hour, Mr. McClanahan," the lawyer answered. "I will have them ready for your signature before the sun goes down."

"Very good," Bobby muttered. "I'm sure my sister will take care of your fee," he added.

"I love you, Bobby," Charlene spoke, unable to hold back her tears.

"You will have to leave, now." It was the voice of a nurse, who just entered the room. "Mr. McClanahan must try to rest."

"And I love you," Bobby whispered, squeezing Charlene's hand.

"I will prepare these papers at once," the attorney said as they left the hospital. "And I will bring them back this evening for Mr. McClanahan's signature."

"That will be fine," Charlene replied. "We will not visit my brother anymore today, for he needs the rest. We will see him in the morning and will be in your office before noon."

The events of the day had taken a toll on both, Joe Ray and Charlene. So they, also, were glad when they were, at last, back in their hotel room.

Just before dawn the next morning, there was a knock on their door.

"Wonder what that crazy Luther wants this time of the morning," Joe Ray was saying to himself so not to awaken Charlene.

"A message for Mrs. Franklin," a tall black man said as Joe Ray opened their door.

"I'm Mrs. Franklin's husband," Joe Ray replied. "I'll see that she gets it. Thank you very much."

Joe Ray unfolded the paper and began to read.

Mrs. Franklin,
I am sorry to inform you that Mr.
McClanahan passed away earlier this
morning. I will be glad to meet with you
before the noon hour today.
                    With Deepest Sympathy,
                    Dr. John Henley

Joe Ray woke Charlene and relayed to her, the bad news.

"Then, we must take him back to the plantation for burial," Charlene said, weeping. "I'm sure he would have wanted it that way."

"We must finish our business at the lawyer's office before we go to the hospital and then, be ready to leave at once," Joe Ray told her.

By noon, all arrangements were made to take Bobby's remains back to the McClanahan plantation and the will the attorney prepared, only hours before, was in Charlene's possession.

"Just one last piece of business to take care of before we leave Atlanta," Joe Ray told Charlene, when they were back at the hotel. "Go on up to the room. I'll be along just as soon as I have a word with Driver Lucas."

When Charlene was far enough away, so as not to hear what was being said, Joe Ray turned to Luther.

"You better have yourself back home before this week

166

ends, or I'll make sure every lawman in the whole state of Georgia knows where you are," he commanded.

"You done caused enough worry for Ole Ben and Mattie, and besides, no one except the home folks know you were the one that robbed that train. I'm sure none of them will ever say anything. And besides, if you stay here in Atlanta much longer, you're sure to wind up in a heap of trouble. Wait here, while I go get Mrs. Franklin, so you can take us to the train station."

Within an hour, Joe Ray and Charlene were ready to board the train for the journey back to Dublin. Bobby's body was in the baggage car. Dr. Henley had seen to that.

"By the end of the week," Joe Ray reminded Luther as the couple stepped aboard.

"Shore 'nough," Luther grunted. "Anyhow, how much yo' reckon dat feller stole, when he robbed dat train, Joe Ray?"

"I'm sure I have no idea," Joe Ray answered as the door to the passenger coach closed behind him.

Chapter Sixteen

The Family Reunion

By the end of the week, Joe Ray and Charlene were back home on the Franklin plantation. Bobby was given a Christian burial and life was back to normal. Charlene decided it was best to spend a few days with her brothers. Joe Ray agreed, because he understood that she and her family needed time together to mourn the loss of their brother.

Both agreed not to tell Ole Ben and Mattie about Luther. They wanted his homecoming to be a surprise.

Joe Ray busied himself overseeing the matters on the plantation, but was anxious for the arrival of Luther. When Saturday passed and there was no word from him, Joe Ray became concerned. He knew that Luther had no fear of him carrying out his threat of turning him over to the authorities.

Near nightfall, Charlene returned from her brothers' place and was also surprised that Luther had not yet found his way out of Atlanta.

"Wonder what happened to him?" she questioned Joe Ray.

"You got me," he answered. "Wouldn't surprise me if he didn't try to hold up another train on his way home. Anyway, Luther must never know what happened to the money taken from the train two years ago. Only you, myself, and Boss Bill share that secret."

"Why don't we have my brothers and all the other folks on their place, over here next Saturday for a barbeque," Charlene suggested. "That will help get all our minds off the loss of Bobby and besides, now that he is gone, there is no reason why our families can't get along."

"Sounds like a great idea to me," Joe Ray agreed. "Let's spread the word that we expect everyone from your brothers' place. We'll make it a two-day affair."

The next few days were filled with preparation of the coming weekend. One could feel the excitement, especially among the black ladies on the Franklin plantation. Because of the bitterness between the two families, the black residents saw little of each other, except at church on Sundays.

Mattie, Sara, and Annie took charge of the food preparation, under Charlene's supervision, of course. Ole Ben and Henry set up tables in the shade of the oak trees surrounding the mansion, and made sure oil was in every torch, so the grounds could be well-lighted after nightfall. Even the black folks who worked the cotton fields helped with the decorations after their day's labor ended.

This was to be a festive occasion indeed, Joe Ray decided. One equal to the gatherings he heard Old Ben and his father talk of having before the Civil War. Most of the week, his mind was on helping Charlene and the others prepare for the coming weekend, but often, he wondered what could have happened to Luther.

"I will go back to Atlanta, next week," he told Charlene. "And this time, I will bring Luther home, myself."

Everyone was up earlier than usual when Saturday morning arrived. When Joe Ray awoke, he could detect the aroma of hickory wood smoke. As he opened the drapes in their bedroom, he could see Old Ben and Henry attending the large pig already roasting on the spit. Snow white cloths already covered the tables that were put in place earlier in the week. Huge vases, filled with flowers, made up each centerpiece. Bright orange and red leaves clung to the gigantic oaks. Even the trees are doing their part to make this a festive occasion, Joe Ray mused and he called to Charlene.

"Better get out of bed before our guests arrive," he said to her. "Looks as if everyone else has been up for hours."

"You should have awakened me earlier," Charlene declared. "I need to be outside helping Mattie."

"Appears to me, Mattie's got everything under control," he answered.

Within the hour, Joe Ray and Charlene joined the others on the lawn. It was only ten in the morning, but some of the guests from the McClanahan plantation were starting to arrive. Large containers of food were placed on the tables. More and more food came with each buggy.

"There's going to be enough food to feed Sherman's army," Joe Ray overheard Mattie tell Ole Ben.

By noon, all the Franklin guests had arrived. Everyone gathered near the tables, ready to partake of the large spread that was set before them.

Joe Ray took Charlene by the hand and led her to one of the tables. "Time to start eating," he said in a voice loud enough to get everyone's attention. "But, I feel that before we do so, I should have Ben ask a blessing."

Strange, Joe Ray thought, having known Old Ben for so long. He couldn't remember ever having heard him pray.

"Thank You, Lord, for lettin' us all be heah, together," Ben began. "An' fer gettin' rid of all the hard feelin's that has been holdin' des fine famly's apart. Bless all dis good eatin's to hep our bodies, an' Lord, please watch 'bout Luther in whatever place Yo' fount suited fer him to be. Amen."

Immediately, upon hearing Amen, everyone began filling their plates with as much food as space would allow. The white folks and blacks, alike, seated themselves together on the lawn, which by this time, was completely shaded by the oaks. Most of the afternoon, Charlene and Joe Ray spent talking with her three brothers, while the black folks caught up on what was happening with their kin.

Just as the evening light was beginning to give way to darkness, Joe Ray saw someone approaching, far in the distance. He watched as the carriage drew nearer, and as

172

the driver made his way onto the front lawn, Joe Ray began to smile. He made his way to where the carriage stopped and extended a hand to the driver.

"This is Lucas," he said. "He's come all the way down here from Atlanta."

The driver stepped from the carriage and removed his hat, a friendly gesture to those who came close enough to greet him.

Mattie got up from where she was sitting on the front steps of the mansion, and walked toward the carriage. When she had gotten within a few feet of where Joe Ray and the driver were standing, she let out a cry that could be heard over the crowd.

"That ain't nobody named Lucas," she bellowed. "That's my baby boy, Luther. Only now, he's growed up some an' got man 'nough to grow him some hair on his face."

"We all thought you wuz dead," she told Luther, hugging him so tight that Joe Ray feared if she did not soon let go, Luther would surely cease breathing.

"Folks said that you wuz de one what robbed dat train some time back," Mattie continued with tears streaming down her weather-beaten face. "But, I always prayed to de Good Lord dat wuzn't so."

"Yo' is right, Mama," Luther lied. "I ain't never had nothin' to do wif robbin' no train."

By this time, Ole Ben made his way to where Luther was standing. He, too, was showing signs of emotion. Try as he would, he could not hide his joyful tears. After all,

Luther was his only child.

"What happened to yo' arm?" Ole Ben asked, after he let go of his own embrace.

"Jus' one of 'em fer-out accidents," Luther began. "I went fishin' one day while I wuz up in 'Lanta, an' I hooked me one of dem big ol' catfish. When I jerked, hit made him so mad, he jerked back so hard, he broke my arm. Reckon hit never did heal up jus' like hit 'sposed to."

Before he could finish spinning the yarn about the catfish, Luther caught sight of Henry Viney and his missus.

"Truth of de matter is, I got shot by mistake," Luther corrected.

"Better try to remember which lie you told to who, if you don't want the real truth to come out, old boy," Joe Ray said.

"Mighty glad to see you again, Lucas," Henry smiled. "Me and the missus been wonderin' whatever happened to you after we left Atlanta."

"My name ain't really Lucas, Mr. Viney," Luther confessed. "I jus' used dat name while I wuz up there in de big city, 'cause it sounds more dign'fied."

"I see your leg made a marvelous recovery since I saw you last, too," Joe Ray teased, still speaking quiet enough so only Luther could hear. "And mind telling me why you are a week late getting here?" he added.

"Hit took me three, four days to sell my horse an' buggy," Luther said. Dey's both old an' nobody wanted to buy 'em. Den after dat ..."

"Never mind," Joe Ray interrupted. "I figure you

174

stopped in Macon and lost all your money in one of them gambling houses."

"How'd yo' know 'bout dat?" Luther asked.

"Don't tell me that's what you really did, Luther?"

"I didn't loose hit all. I still got twenty-two dollars left."

"No, you don't," Joe Ray scolded. "You only got two dollars left, because you are going to give your mama back the twenty dollars you stole from her the first time you went to Macon. And I'm going to stand right here and watch, while you do."

The remainder of the weekend was a joyous time. There were horseshoe games, mumble peg, singing, which included many Negro Spirituals, and renewing old acquaintances, to say nothing of the mountain of food that was consumed.

Luther spent much of his time lying to the other black folks, about what he did while he was in Atlanta, and the rest of the time, trying to straighten out the lies he had already told them.

By Sunday evening, everyone was worn out. Most of the folks from the McClanahan place had already left for home. Henry, Sara, and the others were making sure everything was washed and put back in its proper place.

Joe Ray, Charlene, Ole Ben, Mattie and Luther were seated on the front porch of the mansion, watching the sun melt into the cotton fields.

"Not much better off'n yo' wuz when yo' lef two years ago, are yo', Luther?" Ole Ben questioned.

"'Spose yo're right," Luther answered, "but I still got two dollars and Old Sadie. That is, iffen Joe Ray still lets me claim her."

"Reckon tomorrow, you can start working with everybody else here on the plantation," Joe Ray directed his comment to Luther.

"Reckon so," Luther grunted. "But could I wait 'til nex' day to get started. I shore would like fer me an' yo' to go fishin' t'morrow."

Joe Ray hesitated for a while, weighing his remaining resentment toward Luther for hiding Charlene's letters, against the good times the two of them had while growing up. Not to mention all that Ole Ben and Mattie had done for him and Boss Bill.

"I guess one more day won't matter," Joe Ray said. "Tomorrow, you and I will go fishing."

"Fine thing," Ole Ben said. "I'll have de buggy ready bright an' early, so I can take yo' fellers down to de bend of de river," remembering the many times the two had gone fishing together in days gone by.

"Dey won' be no use in dat," Mattie chimmed. "Dem boys wouldn't think of goin' fishin' lessen dey wuz on de back of Luther's mule."

176